Underwater Dreams

Underwater Dreams

A MODERN GREEK TRAGEDY

James Rouman

Peter E. Randall Publisher LLC
Portsmouth, New Hampshire
2006

ISBN: 1-931807-42-6

Library of Congress Control Number: 2006900198

Peter E. Randall Publisher LLC
Box 4726
Portsmouth, NH 03802
www.perpublisher.com

Jacket Art: William Thomson
Book design: Grace Peirce

— to those persons who ventured over water in search of a dream —

I would like to thank Catherine Bouffides-Walsh for her astute criticism and intelligent suggestions, Richard Clairmont for his attention to language and grammar, and most of all David Whitehead, Chris Grimaldi, Helen Limnios, and John Rouman for their continual encouragement.

Any resemblance to persons, places or events living or dead is coincidental. And although some members of my family and several friends believed I was writing about them, they realized after reading the book that creative memories are a world unto themselves

Contents

Chapter 1   In The Beginning   1
Chapter 2   Paris   9
Chapter 3   At Sea   15
Chapter 4   Initiation   23
Chapter 5   To be or not to be   29
Chapter 6   Discovery   39
Chapter 7   Nexus   51
Chapter 8   Cast of Characters   57
Chapter 9   Reunion   63
Chapter 10   Family Album   75
Chapter 11   Boys   87
Chapter 12   Transition   93
Chapter 13   Stabat Mater   101
Chapter 14   Guy Talk   105
Chapter 15   Caveat Emptor   111
Chapter 16   Downward Spiral   113
Chapter 17   Retreat   121
Chapter 18   Rescue   129
Chapter 19   End Game   133

UNDERWATER DREAMS

1. In The Beginning

*"Seek not, my soul, the life of the immortals, but enjoy
the resources that are within thy reach."* —Pindar

SHE WAS BORN IN A SMALL VILLAGE IN THE SOUTHERN PART OF THE
Peloponnesus in Greece, the only surviving child of the widow
Stamatia. An infant brother had previously died shortly after delivery,
and this birth was cause for concern to those present. Small in weight,
pale and barely moving, she was bundled in wool and set on a table,
a lit candle and an icon of the Virgin Mary beside her. Prayers were
offered by two elderly women in attendance, the room otherwise
hushed as memories of the sibling lost during infancy were recalled.

Slowly, however, the newborn showed increasing signs of life and
within the hour was crying lustily, giving evidence of the power of
prayer and proof of the benevolence of the Mother of God, who was
watching over the proceedings. So said the midwife. It was then that
Stamatia decided to name the girl Soteria—Greek for "salvation," for
it appeared to everyone that the child would survive.

Stamatia had buried her husband, Leonidas, the month before. He
had died, it was generally believed, of heartache and, to some extent,
of shame for having been in America eleven years, returning empty-
handed to a wife he had left behind in pursuit of a fortune that failed
to materialize. He was by all accounts a good man, with some education, but hardly equipped to meet the challenges of a world strange
and cruel to people like him, who could offer only their labor and inno-
cence to others waiting to abuse and manipulate the many immigrants
arriving on the eastern shores. Leonidas had gone to the New World
in 1908, had worked in factories, and had been swindled of the small

fortune he once hoped to bring back. Instead, he returned with nothing to the scorn of Stamatia, who had labored those many years in the olive groves and was now promptly with child. It was a difficult year for the widow, holding fast to her only meaningful possession—the infant she had birthed, and the only one she could ever hope for, having become the latest widow in a village absent of men.

To Stamatia, her daughter was everything, and the bond that developed between them grew steadily as the girl changed from a once fragile figure to the youthful embodiment of all the Greek world could boast. Lula, as Soteria was known by her friends, radiated a beauty and intelligence to anyone in her presence. But as stern and protective as she had been in the care of her daughter, Stamatia was proud to have raised a child seen by others as a rare picture of openness and affection, seeking at times to escape the ever present eyes of a mother who as constant companion stood at arm's length, ready to fend off temptation both real and imagined. An innocent life was Lula's, yet lonely and insular it had to be.

Thus, when Christos came visiting with his father one summer afternoon, dressed in his New World attire and exhibiting the anxiety of a prospector panning for gold, Stamatia felt the same uneasiness she had felt the day of her husband's return. She knew why they had come, for often in those days young men who had acquired a modest nest egg abroad returned with expectations of establishing families with the village girls they hoped to marry.

Numerous young ladies had been delivered to the patriarchal home of Christos's family for the American to meet. But after several failed attempts at finding a suitable spouse, the handsome young man spoke of the limited time he had for courtship and sought the assistance of his father, a respected *archon* of the community, who promptly declared that the widow Stamatia's daughter was the bride-to-be. Although of modest means, yet able to provide a reasonable dowry, the widow was respected and admired for having raised a daughter in the manner dictated by the mores of the times.

At age seventeen, Lula was given by her mother to a virtual stranger, who would take away his bride from the warmth of the Mediterranean sun to the cold of the howling winter winds of Wisconsin. The marriage was celebrated with a banquet in the village square amid tears shed from feelings of both gain and loss.

———

In 1924, the year of Christos and Lula's marriage, an overland journey through the rugged regions of Greece was a punishing experience, making a sea voyage whenever possible the preferred way to travel. Roads were few and poorly developed, whereas motor vehicles, rarely seen, were considered a dangerous means of transportation. Evidence of a fatal accident was often marked along a roadside by a small encasement or windowed box complete with icon and candle standing as solemn reminders of a curve not negotiated or a rocky avalanche encountered. Travel at night was rarely attempted.

The distance between Lula's village, Katavothra (later renamed Metamorphosis), and Monemvasia was short and measured in hours of travel by donkey or on foot. At best it was five kilometers, and not an impossible walk in the summer before the midday sun had peaked. Monemvasia, the fortressed Byzantine city and a seaport of ancient Sparta, was from where the newlyweds were to embark for Piraeus on the first leg of their journey. And it was to that destination that a band of friends and relatives following a wagon loaded with suitcases had come to say good-bye, while singing songs of love and longing.

Determined as she was not to show any emotion, Stamatia broke down at the pier, tearfully hugging and smothering with kisses the obedient daughter who had brought meaning and joy to her otherwise dreary life. And Lula, holding herself tightly against her mother's breast, asked for her blessing as a far-off church bell rang and the shrill horn of the small vessel signaled imminent departure. Christos gently led his wife by the hand onto the ship's deck, where, upon turning to face the assembled well-wishers, she saw for the last time a landscape that would be etched in her memory for years to come.

———

The sea was calm during the overnight trip to Piraeus. Saddened by the ordeal of saying good-bye and wondering if she would ever return, Lula left the deck where for the longest time she had staked out a place to watch the distant lights of the shoreline slowly disappear. On entering their cabin, she saw that Christos was already asleep, breathing heavily as he lay in the upper birth fully clothed, his shoes on the floor below. Lula, likewise, removed her own shoes, placed them alongside her husband's, and covered herself with a blanket on the straw mattress of the lower bunk. She was yet to know the pleasure of sleeping in a man's embrace.

————

The ship was no longer moving. The rhythmic roll of the night sea had ceased, for the vessel was now securely tied to the moorings of a busy harbor. Awakened by the unfamiliar din of peddlers hawking wares, of honking cars and of the endless whine of engines, but most of all of the trampling feet of stevedores in the passageways, the newlyweds arose and greeted each other with an awkward embrace.

"We will have coffee ashore with our friends," Christos said as he combed his thinning hair and helped his bride straighten her dress, disheveled after a night of restless sleep.

"There he is," he shouted as they emerged from the ship, directing the men with their luggage toward a short, dark figure on the pier. "There's Symeon Barros," Christos said as they approached the cigar-smoking man who would accompany them to America.

Barros had come to meet his friends as he said he would. Waving also was his wife, Helen, a stylishly dressed woman from a well-to-do Greek Egyptian family. Symeon had known Christos as a student from their days at the gymnasium in Molaoi, a few kilometers from Katavothra. Born in a neighboring village, he left home as a young man to seek his fortune in Egypt. He lived in Alexandria, where he was involved in the tobacco business. Now he was traveling for the first time to the United States, hoping to find markets for the products he had developed. Barros, a solidly built man, impeccably dressed and with polished nails and shoes, was effusive in his embrace of an old friend as introductions were made and kisses were exchanged among the four.

There was hardly room in the cab to breathe. The suitcases, by necessity, were secured on the roof of the car prompting the distraught driver to state there would be an additional charge for the freight. When he heard he would be appropriately compensated, his demeanor changed as they drove along the dusty road to Athens; and like taxi drivers everywhere, he offered to be an inexpensive guide for the party should his services be required. Aleko was his name. He could be found, he said, outside the entrance to the Hotel Metropole, where his brother was employed as concierge and where, by coincidence, the foursome were booked for the coming days.

As the men spoke of politics and business, the women exchanged stories of their lives and families. Helen felt an immediate connection to the young bride, and recognized instantly she could make this intelligent, but reserved, peasant girl into a princess after a few visits to the boutiques of the city. Wide-eyed and fascinated by the newness of everything around her, Lula was energized as she noted the details of the reception hall, the salons, and the room she was to share with her husband. The hotel was unlike anything she could have imagined in the village, and the sadness that had gripped her until then began to lift. A butterfly was about to emerge from its cocoon.

———

Athens was reeling from the influx of refugees arriving in Greece from Asia Minor following the disastrous war of 1920–22 with Turkey that resulted in the forced exchange of populations between the two countries. Over a million people had been added to a nation barely able to sustain itself after so many of its resources had been exhausted by its earlier involvement in the Balkan Wars and a world war that followed. Yet an air of excitement could be felt by those who visited or lived in the capital city.

And for those from the provinces, the streets congested with noisy cars and horse-drawn carriages, the avenues and shops along boulevards and parks—all constituted a fantasy world to be enjoyed. Sitting majestically on the Acropolis, the Parthenon alone fired the imagination of anyone who knew that at one historical moment Athens had been the center of the universe. The pride Lula felt as she beheld the city below, with Mount Lycabettus in the distance, reaffirmed a promise she had made to herself never to forget she was Greek.

Helen Barros was determined to transform the appearance of the country girl she had just met, and with zeal and in record time accomplished her goal by utilizing the services of the taxi driver Aleko and the bargaining techniques she had mastered while living in Egypt. A woman of good taste with a knowledge of quality and fashion, Helen soon presented Christos with a bride to grace his arm and make him proud to display.

Together, the four spent an evening at a bouzouki taverna hidden along the wharves of Piraeus, where illicit *rembetiko* music of Asia Minor was heard. The following day, by contrast, they attended a performance of *La Traviata* at the Lyric Theater. Swooning at the sound produced by so many instruments, Lula was unaware that in this makeshift production a diva had been singing Violetta in French opposite a tenor singing in Italian, while a local chorus responded in Greek. She was too intoxicated by the activities of the past three days to be concerned about plot or performance. Pleased with everything she had experienced since her marriage, Lula dreamed of Paris and beyond as she listened in the dark with eyes closed and her head against her husband's shoulder.

In the morning she would offer her trousseau to the girl who turned down her bed each evening, wishing her luck in a world far from the mountains of Anatolia, from where she had come seeking refuge.

————

The two-day trip from Piraeus to Marseilles was problematic for the women, who had anticipated an interlude of fine dining on the French ship booked by a travel agent in Athens. A rough sea brought on by a sudden squall had made them sick, leaving the men at loose ends— both reluctant to remain in cramped cabins with ailing wives. Instead, they comforted each other over cognac and snacks; and as Greek men are known to do, they avoided their wives at such moments of need.

The dining room was virtually empty, for the chaos brought about by shifting china and silver amid spilled food and drink was a challenge accepted by only a few stalwarts.

Thoughts of the Atlantic crossing were on the mind of each man as they exchanged stories from their years apart. What would the forthcoming ocean voyage be like? How would the wives fare on the high seas? Was their present shipboard illness a harbinger of things to come? For the husbands, undisturbed by motion, the hours spent together were enjoyable. Christos was eager to hear of Symeon's successes and to tell him of his own.

———

The early-morning sky was filled with seagulls screaming playfully overhead when the vessel arrived. And as the party exited the ship, timid smiles appeared on the faces of the women, who in spite of earlier predictions had survived the voyage. Hesitant at first, they came alive in the bright Mediterranean sun as they scanned the harbor, ignoring their husbands, who were arranging transfer to the railroad station for the overnight ride to Paris. Reasonably conversant in French from his years in the Middle East, Symeon assumed the role of chief negotiator while Christos kept an eye on the luggage. A taxi was engaged to take the party first to a café, where coffee could be taken and other morning rituals performed before locating the railroad station.

The distance from the port to the terminal was short. Once there, Barros insisted that, in order to tour the city, the suitcases be checked through to Paris after receiving assurances from the baggage master of their safe retrieval on arrival. Nevertheless, a certain uneasiness prevented Lula from enjoying the city, as she knew her possessions were consigned to the care of strangers. Was his decision wise or had Symeon been cavalier playing the role of world traveler? Christos appeared less concerned, but Lula said a silent prayer, crossing herself as they entered the awaiting taxi. Hours later, after a dinner of bouillabaisse, the foursome boarded the train, found their compartments, and promptly fell asleep.

2. Paris

*"Life is trouble. Death, No. To live—do you know
what that means? To undo your belt and look for trouble."*
—*Kazantzákis*

WITH NO RESERVATIONS ON ARRIVAL IN PARIS, they looked for a hotel in the vicinity of the railroad station. Their luggage was accounted for and remained under the watchful eye of Christos, while Symeon inquired about places to stay. It was decided the Hotel Bristol, only three avenues away, would be ideal. But ideal for whom? Certainly not for the taxi driver, who when informed of the intended destination made his displeasure known with gestures and words.

"Foreigners, peasants" were the comments heard by Barros, who then placated his adversary with a show of francs and the mention of a sizable *pourboire*. A similar unwelcomed, though more muted, greeting was extended the party at the reception desk when they registered at the hotel. Giving no indication of disapproval toward the newly arrived guests, however, were the porters and chambermaids, who by contrast smiled politely as coins were pressed into their hands.

"Why," asked Lula that evening at dinner, "are people here so cold? Why do they look at us as if they know something about us that we ourselves don't know? Why do they stare and say nothing?"

Symeon drew a breath and began.

"I know from living in Egypt that the French are in many ways the worst people. Italians are warm and happy and will cheat you if they can. The English are cold. But the French act like they don't see you. Like you're invisible and not anywhere in the room. And if it's necessary for them to talk to you—they speak only in French. And if you don't understand them, it doesn't matter. If you are an Arab or from Africa, they treat you even worse.

"And how they smell! We all smell sometimes, but they splash their armpits with cologne—an awful lemon smell—and after a few days it mixes with their own smell and makes you sick to be near them. Why don't they use their noses to smell themselves instead of looking down at everybody with those same noses? Imagine what it's like when they take their pants off! Why do you think so many perfumes are made here in Paris?"

Helen impugned her husband's manners and reminded him that Paris was a beautiful city, inhabited by people who at times did act superior to others. And it was, she believed, because in some ways they were.

"You may not realize," she continued, pointing at Symeon, "that others are offended by the smell of your cigars."

"Those cigars," he countered, "are the reason we are going to America—to sell cigars and tobacco, not perfumes. My tobacco gives us the house we live in and all we have that most other people do not."

Reaching across the table, Helen squeezed her husband's hand and said, "I know I complain about your cigars as you do about the need for bread and butter. I'm sorry. Let's change the subject. If we want to talk about smells, then let's smell the food. Doesn't the *jambon* smell wonderful?"

It was wonderful, they agreed, as Christos poured more wine, and plans for the next day were discussed. Helen, who also spoke French, declared that only in Paris could she find ready-made dresses to her liking. In her mind, the morning's agenda was set. The men would go their way while the women would add to their wardrobes.

Lula was able to purchase only one dress with the money her husband had given her. Yet she reveled in the enchanted world of shops and fashion—a fantasy world of unbelievable choices. Petite and well proportioned, she appeared handsome in everything selected for her to try.

After several hours she was exhausted, however, and wanted to speak to Helen about something that had been troubling her since her wedding night. The opportunity presented itself as they left one boutique and were about to enter another. Suggesting coffee and sweets, Lula was in reality looking for an excuse to talk. They found a table at a café nearby and Lula hesitantly began:

"I don't know how to say this," she said. "I grew up without a brother or a father, and I never saw a naked man until my wedding night. My mother and I never spoke about such things. What men and women did with each other was no mystery to me, but how they did it was and still is."

Lula seemed to focus her gaze beyond Helen, who saw how uneasy the seventeen-year-old appeared and how difficult it was for her to put words together. Reaching for Lula's hand, Helen waited for her companion to continue.

"My mother said my husband would tell me what to do—and that I should always do what he wanted. I was never to say no. It was the husband who had to be pleased by the woman. She told me he would take good care of me if I made him happy."

Lula hesitated and then spoke more slowly, more quietly, looking down as she struggled for words.

"He wants me to leave the lights on so he can see me, and I feel so embarrassed and ashamed. And when he asks if I enjoy what we are doing, I have to lie, for I really do not. I don't know how I am supposed to feel. He tells me to move more, not to be stiff and afraid, to be happy. But I am happy only when he is finished. And after he falls asleep and I look at him and hear him snore, I ask myself, 'Who is this man?' And I wonder how many more times we have to do it before I have a baby."

Lula gradually lifted her eyes and faced Helen, who smiled knowingly, like a priest hearing confession. Helen tried to reassure her.

"*Aman,*" she began, "men are all the same. They have been brought up believing, like their fathers and grandfathers, that to be a man is to be an animal in the bedroom. Let him do as he pleases, my dear, and listen to what your mother told you. One day you might feel different.

For now, be patient and things will get better. But, be careful not to ever enjoy yourself too much or to even pretend to. Christos might think badly of you if you do. You might remind him of some others he has been with before. Myself, I received pleasure only once when I was naked. It was in a *hammam* and from another woman."

Lula wiped her eyes, not understanding what Helen meant. She knew only that she had someone to confide in, and for that she was glad.

Christos and Symeon had been inseparable as students. They studied together, played soccer together, and flirted together with the few girls who, in the early years of the century in Greece, were permitted by their parents to attend school beyond the elementary level. Invariably, the female students were met at the end of the day by a father or brother, who like the teachers themselves sought to prevent untoward advances from some pubescent boy. Hence, any interpersonal contact with the opposite sex was limited to members of one's extended family. As a result, awkward relationships often developed between village boys and girls unable to experience the anonymity that existed in more urban environments.

For Christos, it meant that his early social and sexual interaction with women occurred after he had immigrated to America and with those of a lower class. Although he had been tempted at times to visit a brothel, he chose to remain a novice at lovemaking rather than gain experience in the bed of a whore. Hence, when Christos found a bride and mother for his children, it was clear that intimacy with Lula would test his patience as well as hers. And when Symeon suggested a night on the town without the women, Christos declined, for he knew what Symeon had in mind.

Barros was the more outgoing of the two. Short in stature, muscular, and effusive at times to the point of annoyance, he was always looking for a thrill. For that reason he had left his village in Greece, ending up in Alexandria to live among a population of Europeans, Arabs, Jews, Armenians, and expatriates from throughout the Levant. The city, known for its pleasures and its commerce, was controlled largely by sophisticated and wealthy Greeks. It was there he had gone to build a shop for making cigars and cigarettes utilizing the cheap labor available in Egypt. Aided by money borrowed from bankers, who eagerly gave loans to young and enterprising countrymen, Barros had prospered and taken a wife, while thrusting himself voraciously into the social fabric of the city—often reaching to its darker and seamier recesses.

Christos and Lula were ready and on time for dinner that evening, waiting in the salon for their friends to arrive. When Helen appeared alone in a dress she had hoped would please her husband, it was clear to the others that something was amiss. Upon learning that the two men had not spent the afternoon together playing backgammon, as Symeon had implied they would, she said unflinchingly, "He will come late—or perhaps not at all. Let's eat without him."

3. At Sea

"Happy is he, who like Ulysses has made a glorious voyage."
　　　　　　　　　　　　　　　　　　　　—du Bellay

*T*HEY SAT QUIETLY IN THE COMPARTMENT ON THE WAY TO LE HAVRE. It was called the boat train because passengers were delivered directly to the docks, avoiding the central station in order to expedite the embarkation of ships waiting in the harbor. Moreover, no scheduled stops were part of the four-hour ride from Paris to the seaport, as every person upon boarding had to provide evidence of being ticketed on a steamship—in their case, the Cunard Line's flagship, *Barengaria*. Although the general mood of most people on the train was one of nervous anticipation, the foursome appeared subdued after three hectic days in Paris, and from the wine and cheese consumed en route.

Lula was in a state of reverie. How could she have imagined only a month before then, the world she was now experiencing? From a simple village she had been transported to the storied city of Athens and on to the capital of France. She had traveled by auto, train, and ship and had dined at lavish tables. She visited and shopped at boutiques beautiful beyond belief, and had stepped on paved walks along manicured boulevards among fashionably dressed people.

Christos was thinking of the upcoming days on the vessel that had once been a star attraction of the German maritime services, but was now, as part of war reparations, a possession of Great Britain. Twelve years earlier and still in his teens, he had crossed the Atlantic in steerage class, entering the United States as an immigrant through the halls of Ellis Island. This crossing would be different, for now he was an American citizen booked to travel in an upper-class stateroom with all of the comforts and amenities afforded that status. He was looking forward to a new experience at sea in the company of his wife and friends.

As the train moved inexorably toward its destination, Symeon quietly stared out the window. No effort to engage him in serious conversation was attempted by the others, who were all too aware of the odor of cheap perfume on his clothing. Christos and Lula knowingly eyed each other, while Helen remained remarkably composed. She had not expected a perfect marriage when she accepted Symeon's proposal, understanding that in exchange for a highly charged, though comfortable, existence, she would have to accept his occasional transgression. He was in many ways a good man, she believed, but like her, a person who needed freedom to express himself at times in unpredictable ways.

Excitement was building among the passengers, busily locating parcels and garments as the train continued its slow approach to the awaiting docks. Ahead they saw a monstrous behemoth—a mountain of steel and lights below three rising columns of smoke.

———

Dockside, the scene was one of ordered chaos. The majestic *Barengaria* had arrived that morning from Liverpool and would depart in six hours for New York. Meanwhile, a bevy of dockhands joined forces with members of the crew in rehearsed frenzy preparing for a timely departure. It was like a gigantic orchestra warming up, with each member tuning his instrument before a conductor could raise a baton to create order from cacophony, or so it seemed to those about to enter the bowels of the floating monster—an ark that would transport a thousand passengers to an Ararat in the "New World."

On the pier, people were arriving by the score, anxious to approach the shed where documents and tickets were presented for inspection before permission was given to proceed. They had come by train, private car, limousine, and even horse-drawn carriage with origins primarily from the low countries of northern Europe, France, and Germany. Already on board were many immigrants, largely from Ireland, who had boarded the previous day, and now as seasoned travelers—having crossed the English Channel—were leaning over railings eager to catch glimpses of newcomers to the fold. Scenes of tender embrace, of sadness and joy at the moment of leave-taking abounded wherever one looked.

Excited as they approached the entry shed, the foursome surrendered their documents, which, coded by color, drew the attention of the stewards, who then escorted them to the purser's office and on to their respective cabins. The luggage was delivered by porters who followed close by.

"Lula," Christos said as he put his arm around his wife, "this cabin is small and only a bedroom until we reach New York. But our living room and dining room, our playground, will be the entire ship. It will be our home for now and will bring us to our other one in America."

He kissed her for the first time since they had left Paris, mindful that his bride needed assurance at this important moment. Then hand in hand they left their cabin for the upper deck, where an orchestra was playing and people had assembled to toss paper streamers ashore, all the time waving handkerchiefs at loved ones on the pier below. Suddenly, the three requisite blasts that signaled imminent departure shook the passengers. Their clothing quivered from the bellowing sound. Engine vibrations increased and bells were heard overhead. A jolt was felt as the ship made its first attempt to clear the landing. The voyage had begun.

————

Years ago, a sea lane was the major highway between Europe and North America. It was a pathway known as the Great Atlantic Ferry, a route that traveled a "great circle," or the shortest distance on the globe from one point to another, taking a ship northward from Europe, along the coast of Labrador, downward past Nova Scotia, and on to New York City. Countless human beings boarded super-liners capable of carrying up to three thousand people—crew, businessmen, tourists, and immigrants—to their destinations. At that time, a passenger class called steerage was introduced in which meager, almost primitive conditions were provided to accommodate the hordes of people immigrating to the United States. Others traveling in first and second classes enjoyed amenities comparable to those of a luxury hotel. And so it was for the party of four. For them the days on board the *Barengaria* were a continuation of the good times in Athens and Paris.

The ocean was unusually calm during their crossing, according to the crew. The ship's medical staff encountered few cases of seasickness, and the dining rooms, bars, and salons appeared in continuous play. Aside from taking their meals together and sharing an occasional nightcap, the couples went their separate ways. For Helen, an avid people watcher, the deck became her domain, where, with book in hand and tea within reach, she passed the time while her husband stalked the bars—not so much to drink or cruise, but to regale anyone he could with stories of his business and his past.

The newlyweds preferred whenever possible to be alone, for as it is commonly believed by seamen, the constant and regular motion of a ship, along with vibrations from the engines, induced in women a heightened need for intimacy. And to Christos's surprise, that belief was validated by his wife's increased receptiveness to his advances. They discovered each other and became like the scriptural description of marital union read at their wedding, a new reality of "one flesh."

The end of the crossing was predicted, when late on the ninth day a solitary seagull was seen perched on the railing of the deck where Christos and Lula had been reclining. Recalling the incident at dinner, the young bride was a pleasure for all to observe—particularly their waiter, who, though unable to fully understand what she was saying, had grown fond of Lula and was solicitous of her every wish.

For the couples, the last night at sea was marked by feelings of both sadness and anticipation. Sadness, for they would part after sharing many experiences. Sadness, also, because the past few weeks would never be relived, except as memories. And sadness, too, because they knew they were but two pairs of disparate people charting different courses, like stars whose orbits might never again intersect. At dinner, after coffee and cognac, and before the waiter had been given his gratuities, they recalled their days together and spoke of the day ahead.

"Arriving in New York is an experience one doesn't forget," said

Christos addressing his classmate, hidden behind the smoke cloud his wife was furiously waving away. "When you leave immigration and take your things through customs, your papers must be in order. You will have people there who can help you in either French or Greek. Your tobacco friends should be waiting for you as you go out the gate. Don't buy the Brooklyn Bridge. It's not for sale. Things are different in America. Lots of freedom, but also freedom to cheat and steal. And Helen, remember we are staying at the Rex. Write to us and let us know how you are, and find a Greek church. People there are better than the ones you will meet in taverns and coffee shops."

It was Lula's turn to speak, and with wistful eyes she said, "Symeon, if you ever return to Greece, go to the village and tell my mother, who is lonely and alone, that I am well. Tell her everything. But most of all, tell her I love her and will send for her when I can. Tell her to take care of herself and not to worry about me. I have a good man by my side, and like Jesus, his name is Christos."

"I hope people will buy my tobacco," Barros remarked. "It's the best, but I don't know Americans or what they like. If they don't care for what I am bringing, it won't matter to me. I will have had a good trip, another adventure. But I'll not stay. My Egypt—my roots are deep and difficult to transplant. I am a Greek who must smell the sea, ours with the bluest water and dolphins and octopus. But promise me, Christos: call me if your firstborn is a son, and I will come and be his god-father and give him my name. If it's a girl, never mind."

Helen could no longer remain silent. "A girl becomes a woman only when she is loved by both parents. Otherwise, she remains a child, like many I know. A beautiful, wonderful woman grows like a flower from a seed, but only with care. Do not spoil her beginnings. If you have a daughter, Lula, she can be both yours and mine. I will help you raise her, for I may never have my own."

The orchestra played on. They got up from the table, embraced each other, and left to arrange their belongings. They would meet in the morning before going on deck to witness the arrival.

———

An ocean liner does not simply steam up the Hudson and dock along-side a pier with the same ease as a bus arriving at its terminal. Rather, a series of activities begins when a passenger liner coming from over-seas pauses first at the Ambrose Light Ship, which sits waiting at the southern entrance to New York Harbor. There, a harbor pilot goes on board accompanied by customs and immigration officials, who, during the two hours it takes for the ship to be brought to its designated dock, are busily carry out inspections as a prelude to debarkation.

Much of what happens goes unnoticed by those on board, but at that time searches occur and evidence of contraband, illegal entry, and shipboard illness is sought. Passengers will have been served an early breakfast, instructed to assemble at specified locations, and told their order of exit. Meanwhile, the vessel, under the control of the pilot, is captained first to Ellis Island for the discharging and processing of immigrants before proceeding on to a pier in lower Manhattan.

While in Greece, both couples had visited the American Embassy in Athens for a review of their papers. Symeon and Helen were issued visas, and Lula was given an American passport. Preparing to use the document for the first time, Lula repeatedly uttered the words written on it as if to remind herself who she was. *Sarris* was the word that trou-bled her most. She was unable to understand why she and her hus-band were now called Sarris rather than Sarantarchos, the family name in Greek.

"Sarris means nothing, but Sarantarchos does," she said. Translated, the name means "a forty-year-old nobleman." Again, her husband explained that when he arrived as an immigrant, unable to understand what was asked of him, he became Chris Sarris by the stroke of a pen. The new name sounded more American, he was told. And wasn't that what he had come to this country to become?

Symeon and Helen Barros had no similar issue. Their last name was pure Greek. It also had meaning, and the meaning was "weight" or "fat."

"I like ours better," Christos said, smiling at his wife.

———

Like corks bobbing in a tub of water, the ships lay anchored at distinct distances apart, waiting for the fog to lift so that a safe approach to New York Harbor could be undertaken. At last the *Barengaria,* with her human cargo, was given permission to proceed, and one by one other vessels anchored at the approaches to Ambrose Light Ship were allowed to follow.

Under zero weather conditions all ship movement would cease, but in partial visibility it was considered safe for vessels to slowly ply the Hudson in measured sequence, assisted by foghorn communication and with the help of vigilant lookouts. Radar had not yet been invented.

As the *Barengaria* continued cautiously up the river, her decks began to fill with people eager for a glimpse of America. Little could be seen through the gray mist although overhead the sun threatened to make its presence known. Suddenly, as if on command, and with an accompaniment of bellowing horns, the ship pierced the foggy blanket and emerged from it, allowing the horizon to come into view.

There exposed for all to see was the sight of heaven on earth—the longed-for Mecca, the long-awaited dream, the awesome skyline of New York. A curtain had been raised to reveal a wondrous set design, a city unlike any other, a stage upon which many on deck that day would play significant roles. Lula's heart quickened, as did a hundred others. A collective gasp was heard, for in the distance and to the left, a lofty figure stood majestically holding her torch on high in a beckoning gesture of welcome.

They had arrived.

4. Initiation

"The journey of a thousand miles begins with a single step."
—Lao-tzu

CHRISTOS AND LULA REGISTERED AT THE REX HOTEL immediately after debarking, and by midafternoon were getting back their "land legs" from walking about the city. Venturing out, they carefully counted streets so as not to lose their bearings, maintaining a safe distance from the hotel, which was a refuge in an intimidating sea of people and vehicles. Only by a prolonged stay would they know and appreciate the enormity of New York City. They resolved to return one day. Meanwhile, a letter from Helen Barros was waiting for them at the reception desk. It read, in part:

. . . we came to see you to say good-bye again. We had no trouble leaving the ship and were met by friends, who are taking us to Baltimore, where Symeon has relatives and where we hope to meet with the tobacco merchants. I will always remember the days we spent together and hope your life in America will be happy. Lula, have many children and don't forget me. We love you and know you both love us as well. You also have our address in Egypt and we have yours. When we are situated, you will hear from us. Who knows when we will meet again? God be with you always. . .

They left the following day for Chicago with a transfer to Eagle Creek, knowing the trip would be tiring, all of the sleepers had been booked. It meant sitting most of the thirty hours it would take, with stops in Pittsburg and Cleveland. Lula became ill after their first meal and, sensing she would vomit, rushed repeatedly to the toilet, remaining there until Christos came to inquire after her. She was embarrassed and apologetic, and for the first time since leaving her village felt uneasy about the future. Leaning back as far as the seat would recline, she slept fretfully through the night, refusing in the morning the breakfast her husband suggested.

"Maybe some toast and hot tea will settle your stomach," he said.

"No," she replied emphatically. "I am still nauseated."

She was unaware that she was pregnant.

———

Lula could not hide her distress. Exhausted and unable to lie down, she was afflicted by a nausea that would not leave. And although there were moments of reprieve, she was unable to deceive her husband, who was worried enough to consider getting off the train in search of help. They could continue on later, he said, but Lula opposed the idea. She was anxious for the journey to end.

"How much farther to Chicago?" she asked. "And when will we be home?"

"We have just left Gary, Indiana, and in about two hours will be in Chicago, around noon. But then we must wait for our train to Eagle Creek. Lula, we should go to a hotel where you can rest until we board the train again tonight. In the morning we'll be there and you'll see where I live—not Athens or Paris, but a quiet place to raise a family."

The rented room near the train station was small and sparsely furnished with a bed barely large enough for two. Christos sat in a chair and listened to Lula, who chose to talk as she rested. She asked simple questions and received direct answers in return. Until then, many of her ideas about life in America had been framed through the eyes of others, who saw her marriage as a journey from a simple existence to one of privilege and prosperity.

"Tell me about snow," she began. "I have seen pictures of it on Mount Olympus and from a distance on the slopes of the Taygetus near Sparta. Is it as cold in winter as people say? How long does snow stay on the ground and how can people live indoors all day?"

Christos answered her questions thoughtfully and without hesitation.

"Yes, you will need heavy clothing and covers for your shoes in winter. Yes, you will cook without many of the foods you had in Greece. Sometimes we have things sent from the Diana Grocery on Halsted Street in Chicago, whose salesman visits us regularly and takes our orders. You will miss the fruit and vegetables from your garden. Yes, the figs and almonds come in boxes. And milk will be in bottles at our door in the morning and not from a goat. No, we won't live in a house, but in a flat. What is a flat? You'll see when we get there. We'll find a house some day for us and our children."

"I will miss our church and all the feast days," she said, "and not speaking Greek to the neighbors. You say people are friendly, but how will they get to know me? How can we remain Orthodox if we go to other people's churches?"

The exchange was frank and revealing, and during the needed rest, fictitious notions of each other were tossed aside. She no longer saw him as a swaggering man out to impress, but rather as a person she could lean on and hopefully one day love. For him, she was what he had gone back for. He was returning with a wife who at the moment was nauseated and exhausted.

Although the hotel interlude provided a momentary reprieve from the punishing journey, the overnight ride on the *Hiawatha* continued to torment Lula with its unrelenting starts and stops as it made its way north. At every arrival, Lula awakened, only to fall asleep again after the train had gathered speed, resting all the while against her husband's shoulder.

Suddenly, the morning sun pierced the horizon and refracted a prismatic burst of light through the window and onto the wall. A conductor entered and called out, "Chippewa Junction." It was the name Christos had been waiting to hear; he knew the next stop would be theirs.

"Wake up, Lula. Just a few minutes more," he said.

She yawned as she looked out at the wooded landscape. Trees were everywhere, it seemed.

"What kind of place is this?" she asked herself. "And so flat."

"Eagle Creek," the man finally called out. "I'll help you with your luggage."

The sound of iron wheels against the tracks was piercing to their ears as the train came to a lurching halt. Christos kept his bride from falling forward in the aisle, where they stood anxiously preparing to get off. They had reached the end of the line.

Half-awake, Lula was helped onto the platform. Three suitcases, colorfully adorned with labels of hotels and ships, had been unloaded and ceremoniously placed together awaiting possession. Rubbing her eyes, Lula looked about and saw for the first time the place she would call home.

"Do we call a taxi?" she asked.

"A taxi? There are none," Christos replied. "Here, take the smaller bag. I'll carry the other two."

———

She often longed for the sun and the hot summer days of Greece. She recalled her time in school and the books she had read. She remembered the laughter of classmates and wondered how she had allowed herself to be lifted from the village she knew to a town of five thousand inhabitants in Wisconsin. For Lula, the transition from life in a place of natural beauty to the monotonous landscape of America's northern woods was difficult.

Accustomed to the ever-present chatter of friends, she endured instead isolation and silence until her husband returned from work. Only then would she hear the sound of her voice. More often than not, hers was of necessity an inwardly directed dialogue, a conversation with herself, asking at times whether she was the happy person everyone told her she would be. Haltingly, she addressed her neighbors and endured their laughter whenever she spoke. She was consoled by the weekly arrival of a newspaper from New York, which along with the books procured from Greece was printed in the language she could read. Through all of this, she was sustained by letters from home, which spoke of the need for patience, of the joy of being a good wife, and of ways to care for the son she had recently delivered.

INITIATION

Within a hundred miles of Eagle Creek lived only a handful of Greek families, who from mutual feelings of isolation developed a bond that brought them together at each other's baptisms, weddings, and funerals. Christos and Lula regularly attended those events for the company of Greeks, for news from the "old country," and for a chance to talk about each other's children. And through the sacraments of their faith they became one extended family. So it was when Lula made plans for the baptism of her firstborn.

The son would be named John after Christos's father. Symeon Barros, who once said he would be godfather, was unable to attend. Instead, godparents were found in a neighboring town, and a priest, from two hundred miles away. For a baptismal font, a newly purchased washtub was used, and the rite was performed in the parents' home— a reminder of the way people worshipped in the early days of Christianity, before special buildings were built for prayer. The event was an unqualified success. It was clear to everyone that their hosts had displayed the essence of Greek hospitality expected of them.

For several months after Lula had given birth, she was troubled by irregular spotting. Since her periods had not resumed their clocklike precision, she was treated with pills and potions in an attempt to regulate her menstrual cycle. She had lost the weight gained during pregnancy and now weighed less than before she conceived. Troubled by what he believed was the incompetence of a local practitioner and worried that his wife might be seriously ill, Christos took her to a gynecologist in a nearby city. Upon completing his examination, the specialist delivered an unexpected verdict.

"Stop all medications immediately! Mrs. Sarris, you're pregnant. There is a baby inside you trying to stay alive."

Lula wept on the way home, wondering if she had harmed her unborn child and whether she would ever successfully complete the pregnancy. Would her baby be whole? She prayed to the Mother of God for help, for she had intended no harm to the life she was carrying.

At the appropriate time, another son was born. He appeared

healthy and would be named after Lula's father. He was given the name Leonidas. Leonidas Sarris would be his name.

———

In the early years of the twentieth century, the Soo Line was a railroad company that served the northern part of Wisconsin with a route connecting Sault Sainte Marie, Michigan, and Minneapolis. Between the two points lay numerous small towns, where enterprising Greek immigrant men established themselves in businesses of one kind or another. Brought from Ellis Island to build the locks at Sault Sainte Marie, laborers would ride the trains, eyeing various locales as possible future places to settle in and bring up a family. In that way Christos found Eagle Creek, a town nestled among the lakes and virgin pine forests of the North.

Having spent two years in Escanaba, Michigan working for an uncle, one of the first of the family to come to America, Christos was ready to carve out a life of his own. He decided to plant his roots in Eagle Creek the moment he had stepped off the train. Starting with a Candy Kitchen and then a restaurant, he was soon involved in other ventures that ultimately made him a prosperous and respected citizen of the town.

"How was a young Greek with no formal English education and unfamiliar with the culture of a lumber-based society able to be successful in such a brief period of time?" many people wondered.

The initial years of her marriage were lonely and depressing ones for Lula. She had given birth to sons a year apart and four years later was pregnant again. It was time that her mother join the growing family, for Lula needed help as well as companionship. Stamatia arrived before the delivery of a third son, named Basil, who in Lula's mind would be the last.

The children were brought up bilingually and functioned later as tutors of their parents in the language and ways of the New World. They stayed out of trouble, did well in school, and went on to successful professional careers. Looking back on their boys' achievements, Christos and Lula knew they had done something right: the family was tight-knit and the envy of the community.

5. To Be Or Not To Be

*"No physician, in so far as he is a physician, considers
his own good in what he prescribes, but the good of his
patient; for the true physician is also a ruler having the
human body as a subject, and is not a mere money
maker."*
—*Plato*

IT WAS NOT ORDAINED THAT HE BECOME A PHYSICIAN. There was no
Sarris family tradition that needed to be upheld. And it was not, as
some people believed, a calling predetermined by genetics. Nor had
there been an illness among his relatives or friends for which he felt
compelled to find a cure. It was simply a series of unanticipated circumstances that brought about his admission to medical school.

Leo Sarris was a freshman at Eagle Creek High School when Pearl
Harbor was attacked, and throughout the war that followed, he, like
many others of his generation, was eager to do his part in the effort
that consumed the nation. His greatest concern was whether the con-
flict would be over before he had an opportunity to serve and discover
what lay in the vast world beyond Eagle Creek. Were he to enlist while
still seventeen, he could choose the Navy, which was what he had
planned to do.

In the spring of 1945, the atomic bomb was known to but a few
war planners, and how effective its deployment would be was for many
an unanswered question. Hence, military preparations for the invasion
of Japan proceeded full speed with major consideration given to the role
the Marines would play. To most strategists, the expected ground battle
spelled huge numbers of casualties, which in turn called for the training
of many medical corpsmen. And that is what Leo Sarris became.

While serving his country, Sarris worked as a surgical technician in the operating room of a naval hospital. There he participated in the gamut of activities known to that world, from the duties of an orderly to the functions of a nursing staff and on to the heady responsibilities of assisting during surgery itself. Immersed in the awesome drama of the surgical suite and working with doctors night and day made him realize that they were ordinary people doing extraordinary things— things that he thought one day he could do as well.

In college Leo was a stellar student, which for him meant easy acceptance to the medical school of his choice. For four years he lived and studied at a major medical center in Chicago before serving a rotating internship in Texas.

Feeling in need of a break after his internship, he chose to work on passenger ships as a ship's surgeon at a time when interesting people traveled by sea to interesting places to do interesting things. It was during that exciting year, and in the context of all his past experiences, that he pondered the future. It was then that he decided to become an anesthesiologist, a decision calling for three more years of training.

———

When Leo Sarris graduated from medical school every student was required to serve a rotating internship in order to obtain a license to practice and as a prerequisite to specialty training. The year was spent working primarily in the major areas of medicine, but time was allowed for electives, which gave people interested in specializing an opportunity to sample other fields. It was widely believed at the time that an intern was drawn to a given specialty by the first great teacher encountered, or from exposure to a particular discipline during the initial months of the rotating year. Neither had been the case for Leo.

As a senior medical student, he was nudged toward anesthesiology after hearing a provocative lecture by a psychoanalyst known for his messianic desire to help students find their niche based upon emotional and psychological considerations. And since Freudian theories were vigorously espoused at most schools in the fifties, Dr. Sarris took the psychoanalytic message to heart. After all, he was not from a medical family that could give direction, but instead relied upon instinct, and on what he believed made sense to him. He remembered and took seriously what he had heard.

"From a psychosexual point of view, doctors, in my opinion, differ from other professionals," the professor intoned. "What, for example, makes a person want to deal with another's secretions and delve into the details of someone's bodily functions or other odious things that would likely repel a lawyer or engineer? There is a psychological lesion present, I believe, that is inherent among all who enter medicine.

"And although the lesion may not be recognized early on in medical students, it becomes more apparent later as one sees the specialties these same students choose—or better still—are drawn to. Would a hundred proctologists, for example, have anything in common psychologically? What makes a person want to be a dead man's doctor? What about urologists, who deal with other people's genitals, or gynecologists deciding to exclude males from their practice? Is there a common denominator that exists among baby doctors—or psychiatrists, for that matter?"

In that hour, the psychiatrist offered his opinions as to what draws doctors to various specialties and presented a broad-brush portrayal of the psychological makeup of an array of specialists and their "lesions" as he saw them.

"Be aware that your choices will be determined in part by who you are whether you realize it or not, and that if you understand yourselves well, you will choose a field compatible with your underlying emotional makeup. I want you to be happy in your practice, and therefore offer you my views, having known and interacted over the years with hundreds of doctors and medical students," he said. "Think about what I've said today. See what you do with your own careers and what your classmates, whom you have gotten to know over the past four years, choose to become. Then at some future time look back and decide for yourself whether this lecture made sense."

Leo Sarris could more or less identify with the characterization of the specialist he was thinking of becoming and was determined to learn more. He wanted to meet one of the doctors positioned at the head of an operating table quietly going about his work. He had heard surgeons refer to their "co-pilot" and sought to understand the role that person played during the surgical experience. He made an appointment to speak with an anesthesiologist the following day.

———

"Young man," the older doctor said, "first you gotta realize that a person doesn't come into the hospital primarily to get anesthetized. He comes in to be operated on. And once you get that into your head everything else is easy. In other words, you do your work—and you and everyone else knows it's important, but you accept the fact that you're there only as a necessary evil. If you can take playing second fiddle most of the time, then you might be happy as an anesthesiologist. If you can't, well, then, go into something else.

"You learn to get your kicks quietly and alone in my specialty, because more often than not, only you will know when you've done a good job. The surgeon usually can't really assess how good you are, and bases his opinion of your work on things that sometimes don't mean a hell of a lot. In other words, if his patient is quiet and relaxed and the blood is red, he thinks everything is fine—even when you know that your patient could be in a physiologic mess with those criteria still being met. And sometimes he thinks you're good only because he can push you around or because you never cancel his cases, or worst of all you let him make decisions that are really yours to make.

"And don't expect to walk into a crowded room and hear people say, 'Ah, here comes my anesthesiologist.' It won't happen. So if you need patients to shout hosannas whenever they see you, then become a brain surgeon or something glamorous like that. But if you're into short and intense relationships—the love 'em and leave' em kind—consider doing what I'm doing. To me the patient-doctor relationship talked about in medical school is the most overrated thing I know. Sure, it's often beautiful and gratifying. At other times, it can drive you nuts. With the wrong patient, it can wear you down. The relationship is important, but you can control the extent of it in my specialty.

"So let me tell you something else, young man. We have a connection with our patients no other doctors have. When they're awake we can interact with them before and after surgery as much as we want. And when they're asleep there's a constant dialogue going on between us. They speak to us and we answer back; only the linguistics are different. Our patients talk to us continuously under anesthesia through their blood pressure, heart rate, EKG pattern, eye signs, skin color, body temperature changes, you name it, in all kinds of other ways sending us messages that we have to learn to interpret and respond to. It's almost a spiritual thing that's hard to explain. You have to experience it to understand what I'm talking about.

"Yes, there are downsides. Our work hours are determined by emergencies as well as scheduled cases. Babies come at night. Accidents happen any time of day, and hospital administrators like to keep the O.R.'s working twenty-four/seven. And the practice can be lonely, particularly if you're in a solo practice and there's no colleague to discuss cases with. Sometimes, during a long and boring operation, or when you're working with a slow or putzy surgeon, minutes can seem like hours before a case is finished. But, tell me what kind of practice is perfect. You can't."

Leo Sarris left the anesthesiologist's office with much to think about. He was intrigued and knew he would have to elect a rotation in the specialty during his internship year before he could make the decision he was contemplating.

———

Leo Sarris had known with certainty early on in medical school that he would not be a family doctor as his parents had hoped, for in spite of the broad intellectual challenge afforded by general practice, he rejected it on the premise that everything a family doctor did someone else could probably do better.

And what about the awesome responsibility, he thought, of keeping up-to-date when it is accepted that the half life of one's medical education is no more than ten years? In other words, ten years after graduation, half of everything learned in school would no longer be applicable in one's practice. Leo reasoned that to remain "cutting edge" in medicine, the need for specialization was obvious.

During the month-long elective in anesthesiology he discovered many aspects of the discipline that appealed to him. The moment-to-moment control of someone lying helplessly on the operating table and the awesome responsibility of serving as the external eyes and ears of a human being who had relinquished everything to a virtual stranger suited Leo's nature as a man in tune with the world of a creator. As one assuming the role of guardian angel or of God's right-hand helper, Dr. Sarris recognized he would be conforming to the portrayal of the anesthesiologist once described by the psychoanalyst in his lecture to the senior class. Leo Sarris was a believer—a person who felt that, despite the scientific inferences of evolution, there had to have been a master architect who had ordered the exquisite and known intricacies of the human body as well as those yet to be learned. The concept of a creative force in the universe was not difficult for him to accept.

Moreover, the metaphysical perception of and response to another person's pain, the sensing of a patient's need for blood and nutrients, and the ability to regulate an individual's biochemical environment were some of the action-oriented aspects of anesthesiology that appealed to Leo. And equally important was the opportunity to see immediately the result of one's own efforts.

Likening himself, as he stood alert at the head of the surgical table to a guard, a sentinel, an advocate for the wounded, one positioned between good and evil, between health and harm, Dr. Sarris knew the anesthesiology rotation served during his internship year had led him to the specialty that was right for him.

———

"You want to become what? An anesthesiologist, you say? That's not a doctor, is it? You mean you've gone to school eight years, sailed the high seas for a year after interning, and are now planning three more years just to pour ether like Sister Mary Frances does at Sacred Heart Hospital? Look Leo," his father said, "Your mother and I, all of us here in Eagle Creek, want you to come back and deliver babies, take out tonsils, and look after folks like old Dr. Baker. And fix some bones, too."

Leo Sarris found it difficult explaining his intentions by phone while listening to the disappointed voice of his father, who had always envisioned his son at his side to help write a final chapter in the success story of the Sarris family. But Leo never aspired to own a house on the hill with a Cadillac parked in front. Nor did he see himself in the role of *paterfamilias,* or as a member of the school board, bank board, or any other board, for that matter. More important, he knew that after he had glimpsed the world beyond northern Wisconsin, a life in Eagle Creek was not for him. Yes, he would always remember his origins and appreciate the community that contributed to his persona, but returning there to live was not on his agenda.

"Dad, I know it doesn't make sense to you now. When I'm home on break, we'll talk, and you and Mom will understand. You've got to believe I know what I'm doing. Yes, I'll have an office. A whole hospital will be my office, and I'll be a better doctor for it. You'll see."

He knew his parents would support his decision—hesitantly, perhaps. But he was also aware they realized his decision was part of a leave-taking process, an inevitable one that parents are reluctant to face. Although he was distancing himself from them, Leo was determined that space alone would never separate him from his family.

———

Not long after Leo Sarris had arrived at Hamilton General Hospital to begin his specialty training, he recalled once having appeared before a group of counselors at the conclusion of a three-day period of testing. On the advice of a family friend considered an expert in the guidance field, he had gone to Chicago to undergo an evaluation. As a high school student, he thought he would become a lawyer, but upon discharge from the military he was unsure what career path to pursue. His two-year immersion in the hospital world as a navy corpsman had sparked an interest in medicine, and he was eager to know what "experts" would advise him to do. He wanted to be tested.

"You won't be happy as a doctor," the senior counselor concluded.

"Oh yes, you could do it," he said pointing to a graph. "Your IQ is high enough to get you into and through medical school, and you have the manual dexterity and other attributes desirable in a physician, but you won't be happy,"

Sarris could not believe what he was hearing. "Why won't I be happy?" he asked.

"Because in the preferential choices analysis you did poorly. That is, in the comparative situational questions that were posed, you basically differed every time with the likes and dislikes of a large cohort of doctors already in practice. Remember the test where questions were asked, like: Given a particular situation, would you rather do *a, b,* or *c* ? Well, you seemed to have little in common with doctors out there today. On the basis of the tests we gave you, we recommend that you abandon the idea of studying medicine. You should consider other vocations we have identified as more suitable ones for you."

Shaken by what he heard, Sarris was gratified to know that at least he could become a physician if he chose to do so. Of that he was certain before he had undergone testing. But who was to say what would make a person happy in any given career, or how valid was a recommendation based on the comparison of a nameless group of individuals with another person equally nameless? It made no sense.

"So, what are you telling me? What would I be happiest doing according to your calculations?" Leo asked. The spokesman for the assembled staff replied, "We believe you would be happy as a teacher, high school, maybe college. And you could have a great future as a salesman. Something like a YMCA director would also be a good choice."

Frustrated by what he was hearing, Sarris became angry as the session progressed and it was apparent to him that the trip to Chicago had been a waste of time and money as far as he was concerned. When the session was over, he thanked the counselors, gathered the papers they had ceremoniously prepared, and left.

The grafts, charts, and scores he was given were meant to hold the key to his future, but Leo departed with other ideas, for the experience convinced him of the need to take charge of his own life—to follow his instincts. And in spite of the unexpected outcome, he was determined to return one day to prove that in the case of Leonidas Sarris, the "experts" were wrong.

Not until after he had been in practice a few years, however, did he grasp the flaw in the counselors' reasoning. It was illogical, he concluded, to compare people of one generation with those of another, because unique social conditions and historical events left their stamp on each. It was this truth that had not been factored into the counselors' considerations. Certainly, the interests and choices of the flower children during the sixties could not be compared with those of young adults who came before them or those that followed. And it didn't take Leo Sarris long after his arrival to discover how much he and the diverse group of returning veterans differed from the martinets who ruled Hamilton General Hospital and determined its politics.

Years later Sarris would receive recognition as a pedagogue—not as a high school or college teacher, but as a teacher of medicine. And to the credit of the advisers in Chicago, he did become a convincing salesman marketing his specialty to younger doctors and his hospital as an ideal place to train. He concluded, nonetheless, that guidance counselors should limit their recommendations to informing people what they were capable of doing and refrain from telling them what not to become.

6. Discovery

*"Prayer indeed is good, but while calling on the gods,
a man should himself lend a hand."*   —*Hippocrates*

AT TEACHING HOSPITALS ACROSS THE COUNTRY, the academic year begins on the first day of July, a time when interns and residents, called house-staff officers, arrive for training beyond medical school. Customarily, the outgoing group of doctors spends a day or two acquainting the newcomers with the hospital's physical plant and explaining the management protocols of patients expected to be under their care. At the same time, the neophytes are apprised of quirks, personalities, and expectations of the attending physicians with whom they will work. Meanwhile, interesting exchanges relating particularly to nurses and other hospital personnel occur between the incoming and departing groups. Which nurses, for example, can one learn from and whose judgment can be relied upon? Who performs best in a crisis and who seems more interested in pleasing doctors than in caring for patients? And not to be overlooked, which nurses are available?

Similarly, in those initial days, assessment of the newcomers is made. Who appears to be a bullshit artist, pompous and full of himself? Who is steeped in book learning but appears to lack common sense? Which doctor is capable of listening and learning, and, equally important, who is wearing a wedding ring?

Such was the microcosm Leo Sarris entered on his arrival at Hamilton General Hospital. To his advantage, the time he served in the subordinate role of a navy corpsman had given him knowledge of the often fragile personalities of many people drawn to the hospital world, with its layered fiefdoms. And he was aware of the ever-present grapevine that exists in a community needing no newspaper to disperse gossip both real and imagined.

Dr. Sarris worked hard during his three years as a resident, was an exemplary house-staff officer, and upon completing his training was invited to remain on the attending staff of the hospital he would come to know as his home.

———

Throughout high school and college, Leo Sarris had never fallen in love, or so he believed. He had never had a relationship with any girl to whom he felt totally committed. Perhaps it would be more accurate to say that he had never allowed himself that experience.

He was a popular teenager involved in many activities, and was valedictorian of his high school class. He dated, attended social functions with friends, and was considered a regular guy, one who participated in activities popular among students at the time.

In college, he lost his virginity to an older woman long before the sexual revolution turned sex into an intramural sport, but did not consider himself, as many of his friends thought, a lothario driven by some all-consuming sexual urge. Maybe it was because the act itself had not been experienced within the context of love, but rather approached as a means of expurgation. Perhaps more important things sat on the front burner of his agenda, an agenda that above all included the need to succeed and to please his parents.

The dynamic that existed within the Sarris household was that they believed in some ways they were not only different from, but, better than, most people in Eagle Creek. The knowledge of belonging to a minority was pervasive within the family, for no other in the town could be characterized as such. They were handsome, yet had a look about them that was different from the northern Europeans who comprised the general population. In contrast to the many Poles, Germans and Scandinavians who lived throughout the area, no Italians, Hispanics, Negroes, or Jews had settled in Eagle Creek. There was but one family of Greeks, who might have been considered a minority and seen as a departure from the norm when conversing sometimes in a different language, attending but never joining a church in the community, and often eating unfamiliar foods delivered from Chicago and from as far away as New York.

Although Christos had become a member of the Masonic Order and ultimately grand master of his lodge, he knew that on occasion he was patronized by older businessmen of the community. Lula reluctantly joined the Order of the Eastern Star, only to please her husband.

It was within a narrow and focused mind-set that the Sarris boys grew up. Not to embarrass the family or incur any blemish was the overriding consideration that everyone understood. Whatever would be accomplished, or for that matter was left undone, stood as a measure of the family's Greekness. And by extension, the implication was clear that anything Greek, to some extent, was better—a supposition that, although rarely talked about, applied to women as well. It was a given that Greek girls were brought up differently and would therefore make the best wives. With four men in her household, Lula was heard to say she was waiting to embrace a Greek daughter-in-law as the daughter she never knew.

During high school, the idea of marriage was as far removed from Leo Sarris's mind as the moon. How to avoid being coerced into marriage, as happened to his best friend at a time when abortion was not an easy option, served as the basis for the only lesson in sex education he had ever received.

While in college, getting accepted into medical school was his one imperative. Consequently, he approached dating in a dispassionate way, sanctioning involvement up to a point and cutting loose from any relationship that threatened his equilibrium.

The same was true in medical school, when academic pressures left Leo little time for a vigorous social life. In fact, a married medical student then was a rarity, as many of the choice internships and residencies had prohibitions against marriage as a precondition for acceptance.

Upon receiving his appointment to the medical staff of Hamilton General Hospital, Dr. Sarris knew he had arrived and that the time had come to reinvent himself. The "Greek thing" that had always been important to him now seemed less so, for he knew he was drifting away from his roots. He was determined to approach the future in a more open way. And at long last he felt the need for intimacy.

———

He heard the call for help from the loudspeaker overhead and rose from the table. Leo Sarris left his meal and sprinted to the delivery room, wondering what could possibly be wrong. He had assessed the situation there before going to the cafeteria and was satisfied it would be safe for him to leave. Only one patient was in labor, and not expected to require the services of an anesthesiologist. After all, she had given birth three times before.

Bursting into the delivery room, he saw several people hovering over a pale and lifeless newborn.

"The mother is okay. It's the baby," the nurse said. "We can't get it to breathe."

Telltale evidence of fetal distress was apparent from the greenish brown material on the towel used to wipe the infant. Aspirated meconium, or infant fecal material mixed with amnionic fluid, if drawn into the lungs on a baby's first attempts at breathing, is a leading cause of neonatal morbidity. And that apparently happened when Daisy Butler had given birth to her son, Tyrone.

"How long has it been?" Dr. Leo inquired.

"Six minutes," was the answer.

"Do you hear a heartbeat?"

"Only a weak contraction now and then."

"Here, let me have the baby," he said. Positioning his left hand under the shoulders of the flaccid torso, he allowed the head to fall backward. "Hold it this way and give me a laryngoscope and some suction. Cover him up. He's already cold."

Opening the baby's mouth, Dr. Sarris cleared the oral cavity of meconium. Upon lifting the epiglottis, he saw fecal material exuding from the larynx. With a nurse listening to the infant's chest, Sarris intermittently suctioned the trachea while applying oxygen under gentle pressure as he attempted to evacuate the debris without forcing it farther down the lungs. Periodically, he compressed the chest as others attempted to stimulate the baby by various means.

"Hit the toes hard," he said, "but not the body—no hard spanking."

Finally, the baby moved a hand and appeared to make a fist. And then several weak attempts to breathe were seen as the chest heaved, oh so slightly. The arm muscles began to develop tone, when suddenly a gasp was followed by a feeble cry.

"The heart is coming back. It sounds better—irregular—and I'm counting the rate at about forty," said the nurse listening with a stethoscope. "I think it's picking up even more now."

The delivery room was a scene of tense and hushed activity. Face masks, for the most part, concealed the anxious expressions of those present as all eyes were focused on Sarris, who was trying to evoke a response from the debilitated newborn.

"How's my baby?" the mother asked fearfully. "How's my baby?" she repeated. "Is it a boy? I have three girls. Why don't he cry?"

No one answered.

Holding the patient's hand, a nurse at the head of the delivery table eventually responded, "The heavy bleeding we saw in the labor room was from a separation of your placenta, and the dirty fluid that came out of you at that time told us the baby was in trouble. That's why we had to pull him out in a hurry."

The nurse continued, "But he has a lot of gunk in his chest, and Dr. Sarris is dealing with that now. He's trying to clear the breathing passages so he can get oxygen into the baby's lungs to get him going."

"Who's Dr. Sarris? I don't know any Dr. Sarris."

"He's an anesthesiologist."

Slowly, the newborn came around. He opened his eyes and feebly voiced a decision to live, a sound at first like the chirping of a wounded bird. It was the plaintive cry of one whose future would one day be the stuff of heated debate. Nevertheless, at that moment everyone was relieved to see the infant's color finally turn from an ashen gray to a discernible pink. And after suctioning the baby one last time, Dr. Leo carefully wrapped the newborn in a warm blanket and placed it in an awaiting incubator for transport to the nursery. There, in the coming days, Tyrone Butler would wage his struggle for survival. The day of the neonatal intensive care unit had not yet arrived.

Before Daisy was sent to the recovery room, her obstetrician thanked Leo Sarris repeatedly and said he would call a pediatrician. The nurses went about putting the delivery room back in order, all the while glancing admiringly at their hero.

"I've seen a lot of deliveries in my day, but what you did just now was special," one nurse said.

"Resuscitation is part of what I do," Leo answered.

"If that baby makes it, he'll never know whom to thank. We're brewing some coffee if you care to join us before it gets busy again," the nurse continued. "I just moved here last week from Boston. My name is Martha, Martha Ravitch. What's yours?"

———

Martha Ravitch had arrived from Boston just days before Daisy Butler gave birth to her son, Tyrone. Trained at one of the major medical centers in that city, she was given the task of creating postoperative nursing protocols for patients about to undergo cardiac surgery at Hamilton General Hospital. Her responsibilities were to plan the staffing structure and to provide in-service training for nurses assigned to participate in the new surgical program that was being organized. She was recruited through an agency aware of the work she had done in Boston, and was eager now to begin a new life away from a community that held bittersweet and painful memories.

Martha was adopted as an infant by an elderly Jewish couple, who had provided her a life of comfort and privilege. She knew at an early age of her adoption, and believed her parents when they said she had been chosen by them and should, therefore, consider herself to be a special person. Growing up comfortably in a Boston suburb, she passed through her teens with confidence and with the usual crushes on boys. In school she performed well, motivated by teachers with strong and vital personalities, who later encouraged her to seek admission to a prestigious college for women. There she studied the liberal arts and majored in English literature.

During her junior year, her parents were killed in an automobile accident. Traumatized, alone, and disconnected from her erstwhile world, Martha left school to bury her parents, settle their estate, and grieve—a grief that endured for several years before she could decide the direction her life should take. It was then that she was drawn to a career that would bring her into proximity with others who, like herself, were in need of comfort. She decided to become a nurse.

On one of her hospital rotations, she met a rabbinical student who later became her husband. More than a decade older than Martha, he fulfilled the need for a father figure and taught her the religion her parents had dismissed or practiced only on selected occasions. Her husband would have several years of seminary studies to complete before he could find a congregation to lead. They kept a kosher home, and studied and prayed together, believing their lives were filled with promise and abundant blessings.

That too, however, would not last, for three years into the marriage her husband experienced vague and confusing symptoms. At first, it was weakness and strange sensations in his extremities followed by urinary incontinence. When he began having difficulty swallowing and kept slurring his words, a diagnosis was made of amyotrophic lateral sclerosis, or Lou Gehrig's disease. Martha knew what that meant. It was in effect a sentence of a slow death, for no cure was known to exist.

As the disease progressed to its inexorable end, she left her position at the hospital to become a full-time nurse at home, where she cared for her husband during the tormented, final days of his life. The experience Martha gained from nursing him made her realize the importance of critical care, a new specialized service where in well-equipped venues, one-on-one care is provided by doctors and nurses to acutely ill patients. It was in this area of nursing that Martha would excel and establish her reputation.

If it is true that stress can precipitate illness, then Martha Ravitch was sure to have her share of sickness, for it would be difficult to imagine any one person experiencing more misfortune than she at so young an age. Less than a year after her husband's death, Martha was dealt another blow that altered her life. A gynecologic malignancy was diagnosed requiring the removal of her reproductive organs. Only in her mid-thirties, she found herself without family and with no hope of having one. Desperate for comfort and support, she married a man she barely knew. The marriage was short-lived and a sham. She discovered her second husband was a compulsive gambler and gay. The time had come, or so she believed, to escape whatever curse had been leveled on her life—to turn a page, to look elsewhere. The position at Hamilton General Hospital offered the beginning she was looking for.

———

Tyrone was listed as Baby Butler on the roster of the neonatal unit where Dr. Sarris came almost daily to inquire of the newborn's condition. There, too, Daisy Butler could be seen peering through the glass windows, anxious to know the status of her son. "Come on, Tyrone, you can do it—you can do it," she whispered sometimes. "Move those arms and legs. Cry a little louder. Do it for Mama."

Martha Ravitch would also visit the unit to follow the progress of the boy whose difficult birth she had witnessed. From her observations of the little patient and the data on his chart, she had hopes that Baby Butler would eventually leave the hospital intact and that he had suffered no permanent ill effects at birth.

Leo Sarris was less sanguine in his assessment and shared the pessimism of the pediatricians, who constantly examined Baby Butler for evidence of neurological damage. There appeared to be none, although the possibility of future sequelae existed.

The extensive aspiration pneumonia that was slow to resolve hindered the progress of the infant, who had suffered a significant lack of oxygen at birth. Baby Butler would remain in the hospital long after Daisy was allowed to go home, and in short order became a fixture in the nursery, familiar to many at Hamilton General. While healthy newborns arrived and departed with regularity, one infant's tenure was ensured.

But with time and the aid of loving hands, Baby Butler turned the corner, gaining back the weight he had lost since birth and surprising everyone by his newly acquired vigor. After two months of treatment with antibiotics, steroids, gentle physiotherapy, and the collective support of a dedicated nursing staff, he was ready for release, but only after having left an indelible mark on Martha Ravitch, whose maternal instincts were aroused whenever she held Tyrone.

"You look comfortable in that role," Sarris remarked one day as he saw how carefully she supported the infant in her arms. "I can picture you at home with half a dozen or more to look after," he continued jokingly, unaware Martha would never have a child of her own. "But you'll need a husband to help out. Or are you already married?" he asked.

"No to both," she replied, reflecting on her two previous marriages and not imagining a third. Moreover, the surgery that had left her incapable of having children was a constant reminder that she was not a candidate for motherhood in the conventional way. Yet, Martha knew she could become a mother by a different means, for the idea of adoption entered her mind every time she felt the presence of a baby in her bosom and thought of her own solitary existence. She no longer wanted to live alone.

——

The dream usually recurred during periods of stress. And it always appeared in yellow. Typically, he would find himself in an underwater cave that contained an air bubble large enough to permit him to breathe as the colored waters rushed by. Rarely did he feel anxious, for the notion of entrapment beneath the cascading flow was blunted by the presence of a light overhead, suggesting an escape route should he choose to ascend. Leo Sarris was not troubled by the dream and could not remember when it first appeared. But unlike others that quickly faded from memory, the colored ones were vividly recalled. It was a mystery why a dream had appeared that night, for he was under no stress that he knew.

Sarris rose to answer the phone, which rang relentlessly from the desk on the opposite side of the room. Keeping it there made it

necessary for him to get out of bed in order to respond to the oper-
ator, who each morning engaged him in a briefing calculated to
assess his readiness to face the day. She would tell him what time it
was, what the weather was like, and which cases he was scheduled
for in the operating room. Moreover, she would apprise him of any
important goings-on that occurred during the night, including an
occasional titillating tidbit she was privy to from working at the
switchboard. Her name was Gertrude, and it was only after having
been at Hamilton General several months that Leo discovered she
was fat and older than his mother. Nevertheless, the two bonded
from the early morning exchanges that had become a ritual for both.

Leo Sarris felt rested as he began his shower; he had slept the night
without interruption, a rarity indeed. Only the memory of the yellow
dream lingered. He was not expected in surgery until nine, allowing
for a leisurely breakfast and the opportunity to review his notes for the
clinical conference scheduled that afternoon. But first he wanted to visit
the nursery.

———

Now a well-nourished boy, Tyrone Butler was ready for discharge from
the hospital. His mother came to the nursery daily to hold and feed
her son, and by so doing earned the respect of the nursing staff, who,
although pleased by what had been accomplished for the boy, were sad
to see him go. Daisy was praised and told she should consider someday
becoming a nurse's aide. No one doubted her parenting skills.

Among those who had come that morning to say good-bye was
Martha Ravitch.

"You have my phone number and address, Daisy. Don't hesitate to
call me anytime. I want to help if you need me," she said as she
embraced both mother and child with one enveloping hug.

To those who had walked her to the cab, Daisy replied, "You all—
everybody here been so good to me. I won't forget. Jesus sent you, I
know. Thank you, Jesus," she sighed as she wiped her eyes.

"Miss Martha," she continued, "when I be settled, I clean for you.
Anything I can do for you, too, I will—you know I will. And don't

forget what we talk about. Get yourself a baby—you hear? We all need somebody."

She waved as her car drove away.

———

Daisy and Martha had often spoken about the challenge of raising a child as a single parent. And during their discussions, Martha wondered if her friend's last pregnancy had been accidental or a deliberate gamble on her part to have a boy. Whatever the case, it was clear that Daisy was happy and not intimidated by the problems posed in "going it alone." That much Martha could see. They met in the cafeteria after Daisy's visits to the clinic when she would call Martha, who responded if her schedule allowed. Martha's shift ended at four.

For several years, Daisy Butler had an on-and-off again relationship with Tyrone's father, a man who seldom worked but who was always an eager recipient of Daisy's generosity. And when periodically he did hold down a job, his monetary contributions to the support of the household he considered himself a part of were trivial. At best, he was "company" for Daisy, who alone kept her family together with help from public agencies and from the income she earned working as a cleaning woman. Essentially, she had been a single parent most of her adult life. Her luck with men was abysmal.

"I was tired and angry when I finally put him out of the house. We didn't need to divorce, cuz we never married," Daisy said. "I was tired of his drinkin,' his foul mouth. When I realize all he wanted was sex and a place to stay and a place to eat, I knew he jess like the others, nothin' for me but an old plug. Too much arguin'. Too much nastiness. He put me down all the time. Yep, he kept me down. He say I change a lot, but I say I jess woke up."

Daisy Butler had asked a sister to move in to be the sitter for her children when she would resume working again, for now she was free of the man who had long been a burden. She had her daughters, her clients, a few friends like Martha, and at last her son. Martha was struck by the confidence Daisy displayed as she left the hospital and marveled at the change apparent in her friend. A baby boy, it seems, had made the difference.

"Miss Martha, you need a baby too," Daisy kept repeating. "I know you do. You be a good mother. You say you can't have children, but you can. Give a home to a poor orphan. Take a baby some woman don't want and make it your own. You say you don't need another husband; well, you don't say you want no family. Watchin' you, I know you do. I know you want a baby. You have so much to give. I don't mean jess money and things. I mean love. Love you gives and love you takes back."

She had struck a nerve, for as unsophisticated as Daisy was, she sensed the loneliness of the nurse who through their visits had become a confidante and friend. It was the old refrain. The repeated allusions to motherhood, interjected initially as simple melodic statements, were developing into a chorus that would not be hushed. Daisy had planted a seed, and in Martha's mind the idea had begun to grow.

7. Nexus

WHAT WOULD PEOPLE SAY? WHAT WOULD THEY THINK? Martha had always been sensitive to the opinions of others, and as the idea was taking shape in her mind to join Daisy Butler in the sorority of single motherhood, she found herself ambivalent about what to do. By adopting a baby, she knew that praise would be heaped on her by many friends, and that others would only question her motives.

Martha had often wondered what her own biological parents were like. She was aware that many scientists believed personality and temperament were to some extent inherited and that nature played a role, as did nurture, in shaping character. This she understood from studies of identical twins separated at birth who when examined years later were found in many ways to strongly resemble each other, sending behavioral scientists reeling as older theories of development were challenged. She appreciated the fact that her adoptive parents had taken a chance on the quality of her own DNA. They had gambled and won, she believed. Now, wasn't it her turn to consider doing the same?

Martha's frequent visits to see Tyrone Butler in the nursery had served as a respite from the high-wire existence of intensive care nursing. She was invigorated each time by an awareness of the promise of a better future for its little inhabitants in stark contrast to the hopelessness that was the lot of many of her patients, often at the opposite end of life's spectrum.

As a nursing supervisor, she was sometimes called upon to fill in for others and to work overtime when absenteeism made it necessary. On such occasions when a need arose in the delivery room, she volunteered to substitute there in order to experience vicariously the joy of giving birth.

And when she pondered the restrictive nature of her work, she felt abused at times by the demands placed on her and sought some form of reward besides the gratification derived from helping others. The hospital itself, she believed, was a cauldron, a place where life and energy were extracted from the willing bodies of its staff and gifted to those in need. Her existence was one of service—rewarding, yes, but begging for some new dimension.

"Dinner and a movie sound great to me," she replied when Dr. Leo Sarris called for a date. "Yes, I'm free Wednesday night. I'll be ready at six."

———

Wednesday was Martha's day, a day to run errands, pay bills, and shop for food. On Wednesdays she had time to think and regroup from the demands of work, time to add to the verses in her book. She loved to write. Today she wanted her home to appear inviting. She was seeing Leo Sarris, a man she worked with but hardly knew. They had spoken occasionally in the intensive care unit, but only briefly. He arrived promptly at six and was offered a glass of wine.

"I have a cabernet. I'd say you were a red wine man. Am I right?"

"Red's fine," he answered. "Will you join me?"

She peeled the lead seal off the neck of the bottle, inserted the opener, and pulled on the cork.

"Damn it. I always break it off with this opener. What am I doing wrong?"

"It's not the opener," Leo answered. "Here, let me have it. Look, you've got to get the screw all the way into the cork. See how easy? Now to get the rest out without pushing it back into the bottle. There, I've got it."

They drank and they talked. He traced his steps from Eagle Creek through medical school and on to Hamilton General. She in turn recalled her life in the Boston area, her marriages, and the events that led to her present job. They spoke about people who worked at the hospital. She took shots at doctors, many of whom had much to learn—even from nurses, she said. He countered by calling attention to some of her colleagues who in his opinion were good at fluffing pillows and not much else. They laughed and finished the bottle before taking aim at each other.

"I'll go first now that we've demolished the hospital staff," he said. "When I first met you, I thought you had no sense of humor until I realized what made you tick. It's about good nursing and not winning a personality contest, isn't it? It means putting the patient first. But for some of you nurses, it's more about being Miss Congeniality."

He got up from the chair and yawned, stretching his arms in the air before sitting down again to continue their conversation. They talked about Daisy Butler and how caring for her and her son had made them notice each other.

"I like Daisy," Martha said. "She's really a good person and fun to be around. She's taught me a lot about myself and given me something to think about. She's going to clean for me. God knows I need help— just look at this place."

As they spoke, each was aware an examination was being conducted by the other—he, to determine her probable age, and she, to assess his overall physicality. He was in good shape, and that pleased her. Women could be soft, she believed, but not men.

From the litany she recited of the events in her life, he calculated in his mind she was still in her thirties and probably a few years his senior. But that was of no concern to him. She was, he believed, a take-charge kind of woman, and he liked what he saw.

"What are you in the mood for—Italian or Chinese? I haven't made a reservation."

"I could eat anything," she said, "but I'll pass on the movie. I'd probably sleep through it anyway. Are you all right to drive?"

They put on their coats, closed the door behind them, and walked to the car. Leo's appetite had grown, but not for food alone. The evening had gone well and he knew there would be others. He had found a friend, someone he could relate to. Martha, on the other hand, had experienced similar feelings before, feelings felt at the first blush of a new acquaintance and from the easy rapport brought on by wine. But she also thought something might develop beyond this first encounter.

———

Over the next few weeks, they occasionally saw each other in the intensive care unit, although the cafeteria was the scene of most of their encounters. There, one day after a hastily eaten meal, Leo asked Martha if he could interest her in dinner and perhaps a movie.

"You've already taken me out once. Remember? It's my turn now. So, why don't you come by some night and I'll fix something," was her reply.

"Sure, I'd like that, and I won't even ask if you can cook. I'll take my chances."

"We have a date then," Martha answered, "but give me some lead time so I can make something special. And just for the record, I can cook."

Aware that Leo was of Greek descent, Martha decided to surprise him with a few dishes she had learned to make from relatives who were also of Eastern Mediterranean origin. For the occasion she prepared stuffed grape leaves and an egg-lemon chicken soup—both staples of the Greek cuisine. But her *pièce de résistance* was the lamb roast, slowly cooked, well done, seasoned heavily with garlic and oregano and basted with a lemon, basil, olive oil mix. No rare lamb with mint jelly. That was for Anglo-Saxon palates.

"I feel like I've died and gone to heaven," Leo said as he entered her apartment. He recognized an aroma from special occasions in Eagle Creek when his mother and grandmother celebrated their ethnicity during religious holidays and whenever certain people visited.

"I'm sorry," he said, "but the bottle of wine I have with me will hardly be adequate for the meal you've prepared. I should have gotten something better."

"Nonsense," she answered.

They ate. They talked and laughed, recalling incidents in their past.

He mentioned his family and the circumstances that led to his entering medicine. She spoke openly of being adopted and how empty her life felt now as an orphan with no prospects of having children. He saw her as someone emotionally unfulfilled, yet searching. She recognized his sensitivity and an ability to listen—qualities not learned, innately possessed by only a few. "How rare he seems," she thought. "It's a pity his patients are usually asleep."

When the bottle was empty and standing on its head, she decided to apprise him of her plans. "Will you think I'm crazy if I tell you I want to adopt a baby?" she began. "Or will you lecture me on the importance of a child having two parents instead of one? Do I care if people think I'm selfish and concerned only about myself? Not really. The simple truth is, I want to be a mother. I want the experience of raising a child and having a family. Why shouldn't I?"

Leo saw the same determined expression on Martha's face he recognized whenever she responded to a medical emergency. This was serious business, no doubt about it. Yet, he felt compelled to play the devil's advocate.

"I'm sure you've thought it through. Adoption isn't like trying something on for size, or seeing whether or not you like what you've done. It's final. You've bought it. And you can't send the goods back if you think you've made a mistake. So, why am I telling you all this, anyway?"

After a lengthy discussion, Leo knew he had not shaken her resolve; for she smiled and said she had heard all of the arguments before.

"Well, then, I guess if anyone can make it work, you can. So if it fills a void in your life, do it."

"If I get a boy," she continued, "there'll be times when he'd need the influence of a man in his life, and I wouldn't mind if that person were someone like you."

"I'm flattered," Leo said. "But how can you be sure I could influence him or be any kind of a role model for your yet-to-be-delivered kid, if that's what you're asking? You hardly know me."

"Good point. I don't know you. I'm just fantasizing. What I'm trying to say is that if I adopt a boy, he'd need a father figure growing up. Right? Who knows, maybe by then I'd have found out you were some kind of jerk and wouldn't want you in the picture anyway. Not to worry just now."

"By then," Leo countered, "it's anybody's guess where either of us might be. Keep dreaming. No harm in it. That's what you should be doing—thinking and planning ahead."

"Dr. Sarris, all kidding aside, from what I've seen of you I'm sure you'd fit the bill. But hey, I'm not asking for a commitment."

Whatever the case, Leo was pleased he was being factored into Martha's hypothetical family equation, and was enjoying the give-and-take of their conversation. It had been a good evening. "A gutsy woman," he thought to himself. "She deserves all the help she can get. She'll certainly need it."

"Martha, haven't we agreed that away from work you'd call me Leo? So cut the doctor stuff, at least until such time when you might want to refer to me as daddy," he said teasingly. "Boy or girl, whatever you manage to get, you can count on me."

He thanked her for dinner as she walked him to the door. She was surprised when he kissed her on the cheek.

8. Cast of Characters

*"In the creative process there is the father, the author
of the play; the mother, the actor pregnant with the part;
and the child, the role to be born."*   —*Stanislavski*

MARTHA KNEW WHAT SHE WANTED. How to proceed was the question. Should she speak to her gynecologist, who was also a busy obstetrician? Were there agencies that would take her seriously, or should she consult a lawyer first? Wherever she turned and whomever she asked about a course of action, there was resistance from those who questioned whether she understood the responsibility of it all. What would people say? Raising a child alone is not something most people would willingly undertake. Yes, death and divorce sometimes inflict the burden of single parenthood on women, while an illegitimate birth often does the same. But to elect to be in that situation is not the norm. In Martha's mind, however, her case was different. And once decided, she would not be deterred.

She had heard through the hospital grapevine that private adoption was occasionally arranged by physicians when an unwanted pregnancy was considered "choice"—that is, when an attractive physical yield was expected and made available for a friend. She knew such events were rare and could not be counted on. Less "desirable" unwanted newborns, on the other hand, were given over to agencies with lists of couples waiting to adopt. Those agencies in turn imposed strict criteria for determining which households met their requirements. Martha also learned that an unmarried, middle-aged woman received scant consideration from a reputable agency and that religious institutions were particularly restrictive in their placement of children.

Where to turn next? A lawyer, perhaps? But which one? In the Yellow Pages, she found an attorney who practiced "family law," and placed a call, only to be told what she already knew: namely, that any legitimate agency would deem hers a hopeless situation. He suggested, however, that she come to his office if she were willing to consider an overseas adoption, which in his opinion was her only option. But he warned that the process could be expensive and might require a lengthy stay in a foreign country. She would have to deal with local politicians and sometimes unsavory people as well.

"It can be done," he said. "And I'll help you. But you have to know what you're getting into. It won't be easy and it'll be frustrating. Just how badly do you want to be a mother, anyway?" he asked.

"Badly," she replied. "Just tell me what I have to do."

——

"You can be a mother right now," he said as he ushered her into his office. "That is, if you'll accept an older child or one with special needs. But, as I said yesterday on the phone, a newborn is out of the question. All the agencies I deal with tell me the same thing. If you want a baby you'll have to go out of the country. And with your dark hair and complexion, I'd say Central or South America is where you should look. What nationality are you, anyway?"

"I don't know," Martha said. "I was adopted, too; but I was raised by Jewish parents, whose folks came from a part of northern Greece called Epirus—from a group of people called the Romaniotes, who lived there since before Christ. Some people say they were one of the lost tribes of Israel. When my parents got me, they were told I was either Portuguese or Italian, from the Providence, Rhode Island area. The truth is, I don't know what I am."

"I never heard of the people you're talking about," the lawyer replied. "How are they different from those forced out of the Iberian Peninsula during the Inquisition, the Sephardic Jews?"

"The Romaniotes were a very much smaller group, and over the years were well integrated into the Greek population because they had no special language of their own, like the Jews from Spain and Portugal who spoke Ladino. Why am I telling you all of this?" she asked. "Maybe it's because I've often thought of having a little Greek baby. It would make me feel like I was giving something back."

The lawyer's name was Lofton. He was large-bodied, lanky, big-boned, and bald. And although his appearance seemed threatening for some people, he spoke softly with measured words, suggesting that he had a real interest in his clients' problems, which in fact he did.

"I don't know anything about Greece, but I do know about Nicaragua. I have contacts there, and I've arranged several adoptions recently. If you're interested, I'll see what I can do."

"Yes, of course, I'm interested. That's why I'm here," Martha said. "Just how complicated is the whole process? How much time off from work would I need?"

"It could go fast or you might have to spend as much as a month there. But I'll touch base with my people and ask them not to involve us in anything that's likely to become a prolonged hassle. If everything goes well, here's the deal. Before you leave, I'll have made all the arrangements including those necessary to obtain an American pass-port for the baby. By the way, have in mind a name for both a boy or a girl, which will be filled in on the papers down there when we know what we have.

"A lawyer in Managua I work with takes care of things at that end. And by that I mean payoffs to officials, agencies, and parents if we get a baby directly from a mother. Older children from orphanages are plenty, but we want a baby, an infant, right?

"For now, here's what you need to pay me up front so I can get the ball rolling. We'll settle the final amount when you return. Go back to work. Buy an open round-trip ticket and be ready to leave in a hurry. It may take time or you could hear from me tomorrow. Fill out these papers and get them to me right away. I'll need to send information about you to my contacts. If you have any questions, call me. But just remember. The process could be expensive. You'll have to take plenty of cash with you because even though you think you've covered all your expenses before you leave, there will be others. Trust me."

She thanked the lawyer and left his office elated by what had been accomplished, all the while aware of skipped beats in her neck from the adrenaline rush she was experiencing.

———

Martha was deep in thought during the flight from Managua to Miami, glancing occasionally at the son she had registered the day before at the American Embassy in Nicaragua. In her possession was the prize she had long sought. Once aloft, the baby had fallen asleep in the empty seat next to hers until turbulence prompted him to cry. And cry he did, uncontrollably and for the longest time. When a cruising altitude had been reached, young Evan Ravitch was quiet again.

Prior to takeoff, Martha had put two drops of a medicine into his bottle. Good for colic, the potion was used by the indigenous mestizo population to sedate colicky infants. For Martha, the result afforded a much needed rest. For Evan, it was his introduction to drugs. With the infant at her side, she recapped in her mind the events of the past week.

Martha had arrived in Nicaragua following a hasty departure and was met at the airport by Señora Flores, the lawyer who was to expedite the procurement process in Managua. On the way to the hotel where accommodations had been reserved, Señora Flores stressed the need to move quickly because the mother, who had agreed to give up her child, was seriously ill. An emergency cesarean section had been performed, and now three days later the patient was feverish from infection, the result of a complicated labor. Were the mother to die before the necessary legalities had been completed, the adoption could not take place. There was no time to lose—no time to eat, nap or freshen up. There was business to take care of.

They walked to an office near the hotel, where an elderly man was waiting. The father of Señora Flores and a lawyer himself, he was prepared to deal with the hospital, the local officials, and the parents as well. The first step, he said, was to visit the municipal offices for documents giving permission to remove the child from the hospital. Then, on to the U.S. Embassy, where a passport, using a photograph of the infant taken at the hospital the day before, would be issued in the name of Evan Ravitch. And to facilitate matters, the lawyers asked for an additional five hundred American dollars. Given as reason was the urgency of the situation and a need to assuage certain officials.

Noisy street vendors, honking cars, and animated voices set the stage as the party arrived at the hospital, a two-story building located in the heart of the city's business district. Told to remain in the hallway, Martha watched as Señora Flores and her father entered a room, where a middle-aged man and several children hovered over a pale woman who appeared to be asleep. The children were asked to leave when the mother was informed that the party she was expecting had arrived. With a look of resignation, she signed several papers and in turn received an envelope, which she promptly gave to the man at her bedside. Outside the room, Martha observed the children she believed were siblings of the child that would soon be hers. Pleased by their attractive features and well-proportioned bodies, she hoped one day Evan would look like them.

Señora Flores jovially greeted doctors and nurses on the way to the nursery. There, after inspecting the documents presented to her, an elderly nurse departed and soon returned holding a baby bundled in white, with only black hair showing atop a red face. And as if performing a solemn liturgical ritual, she placed the child in the arms of the expectant mother, who, overcome with emotion, wept silently. Not wanting to intrude on a private moment, the others left so that Martha could experience for the first time her infant's breath against her own.

The plane landed on schedule, and as promised Daisy Butler was waiting at the airport. "A fine-lookin' baby," she remarked. "Now we got work to do."

9. Reunion

"What is a friend? A single soul living in two bodies."
—-Aristotle

LULA AND HER MOTHER OFTEN THOUGHT OF GREECE and the simple life they had left behind. During the brutal winter weather, when snow was measured in feet and temperatures dipped below zero, they wondered what planet they had come to. Yet the idea of questioning a decision made years ago was never voiced by mother or daughter. Disagreements between Christos and his bride were rare, for it was clear he would be deferred to. Things were as they were and Stamatia was there for Martha to lean on.

With her mother's help, Lula's house was spotlessly clean, and a place where coffee and sweets were offered to anyone venturing by. The milkman and mail carrier in particular received special attention from the women, whose eagerness to chat bespoke a certain loneliness.

Once during the Depression years, Christos came home to find the ladies of the house serving a vagrant in the dining room—a man who had appeared at the back door asking for food. Over that event Christos exploded, and denounced their hospitality as extreme. *Philoxenia,* the Greek word used to denote hospitality but that in reality translates as "love of a stranger," had been taken too far. Although he appeared angry, Lula knew her husband secretly applauded the gesture, for he too was inured to a custom known to Greeks since antiquity. As one reads in Homer's *Odyssey,* it was not uncommon for a traveler to be bathed, clothed, and even fed before being asked his name or the purpose of his visit.

Lula came to enjoy life more in Eagle Creek as her boys were growing up, taking pride in their accomplishments while embracing a world seen through their eyes. The oldest son was the serious student who served as the conscience of the other two. The youngest and largest represented the family on the athletic field; Leo, the middle one, was the actor and at times a charismatic scoundrel.

The boys worked during their vacations "to develop respect for money," as their father put it. They served as acolytes of St. Barnabas Episcopal Church, but never received its sacraments; the "true faith" was preserved by the Greek Orthodox Church, or so everyone in the Sarris household believed. That assumption, however, did not keep Lula from joining the women's guild or participating in its activities. Although she had joined the Order of the Eastern Star and abhorred its ritual, which she found silly and a poor substitute for a well-conducted liturgical service, she understood that social acceptance in Eagle Creek was bestowed by the ladies of the lodge, and that their annual Christmas dance was the highpoint of the social season, such as it was.

Christos was happy and never hesitated to tell friends he knew what he was doing when he journeyed to Greece to find a bride. "We didn't have a Hollywood-type romance before we married, but Lula learned from her mother what she had to do to make me happy, and I knew what was expected of me. It was old-fashioned, but over there people understand those things. Mothers tell their daughters where their places are, and that's why we Greeks don't have as many divorces as others do. People here complain about their mother-in-laws, but not me. I've got a good one. She works harder than any housekeeper ever would. But most of all, she keeps my wife from being too homesick."

Money did not grow on trees in America, as many immigrants had believed, but for Christos it might just as well have, as the opportunities to make money over the years were many. Smitten by losses in the crash of 1929, he concluded that the stock market was no more than a gambling casino for people removed from the centers of commerce and with no access to good advice. From then on, he purchased only things he could see and touch or put into his pocket. His first investment was the house they lived in, which was just one of several properties he later bought and sold.

And then he discovered land. Coming from Greece, where it was at a premium in the mountainous reaches of the Peloponnese, he was astonished to learn that parcels stripped of trees could be purchased for very little. This he systematically proceeded to do, predicting the land then considered worthless would one day command a price greater than when it was purchased. All he would have to do was wait.

Christos was also a shrewd merchant and a poker player at closing a deal. He knew when to fold and when to draw. Timing and a straight face defined his strategy. He worked hard at his business enterprises and over the years spent hours on the run, returning home with little or no time for the women of the house. He was on a treadmill and he knew it. But when asked to slow his pace, he answered that he had three sons to educate, and that took money. He considered himself a good provider, but his neglect of Lula, though not intentional, was real. He had given her everything he believed she wanted: a well-appointed home, clothing that few women in Eagle Creek possessed, jewelry, and a fur coat for special occasions. She was in her fifties, still beautiful, with money to spend, but in need of attention.

What she wished from Christos, more than the material things he provided, was greater intimacy— intimacy with the father of the sons she had raised. She wanted to know she was desired. Instead, she found herself more often alone with an ageing mother, who could only advise patience.

Lula reached for the phone one afternoon, her nap interrupted. Slowly sitting up, she carefully positioned the receiver on her ear before answering.

"Who is it?" she asked. "We have a bad connection. Helen? Helen who? Oh, my God! Helen Barros. Helen, where are you? Of course you can come by."

———

For several years after coming to the United States, the two women had kept in touch, primarily during holidays and by mail. A long-distance call was considered a luxury to most people at that time. In the beginning, Lula wrote regularly to Helen describing her rapidly growing family and telling her of the arrival of Stamatia, without whom, she said, she never could have coped. She spoke of her husband's business ventures, though it was clear she understood little of what he was doing.

Her life gradually evolved into a predictable routine of small-town, middle-class living, sparked occasionally by the unexpected appearance of Greek-speaking people passing through. Usually, it was a traveling salesman or a family from some neighboring town, bringing along children to be compared with those of Christos and Lula. It did not matter that the offspring of both families were barely pubescent; in the minds of their parents, it was never too early to think about matchmaking. Such occasions calling for traditional expressions of Greek hospitality provided a ready podium for Stamatia to hold forth in the language she claimed everyone was forgetting. After a few years had passed, however, contact between Lula and Helen ceased—not intentionally, but through simple neglect.

Helen Barros had no difficulty adjusting to living in Baltimore, where a Greek social presence existed long before her arrival. Although her life there hardly approached in sophistication the one she had known in Alexandria, it was, for the most part, tolerable. She was near enough to Philadelphia and New York City to shop for objects needed to furnish the large house she had purchased. And without children to occupy her time, Helen spent most days alone, as her husband often found it necessary to travel on business, or so she was led to believe.

The New World had been good to Symeon Barros. He understood quickly that importing tobacco into a country with an abundant supply of its own held no promise of prosperity. But having become acquainted with many of the shop owners he had hoped to supply, Symeon realized he could provide them with other goods they needed. An engaging salesman, he cultivated his clients as zealously as he would a newly planted garden, and was able in no time to acquire a building to house the items marketed by his firm, now called Atlas Products.

As his business grew, so did his absences from home, leaving Helen alone more often than she thought necessary. To their friends they appeared to have everything, but Helen had grown restless and increasingly indifferent to her husband. So it was when Lula learned of Helen's impending arrival.

Symeon and Helen Barros led separate lives in Baltimore. He was the businessman frequently absent from home. She was left to pursue interests of her own. In the initial years following their arrival, they attended church regularly, and as new additions to the community were habitual guests at parties, weddings, and baptisms throughout the area. But finding it increasingly difficult to reciprocate as time went by, they slowly became disengaged from friends and relied more and more on themselves to find outlets for their nervous energies. Gregarious by nature, Helen felt the isolation more than did her husband, whose travels offered him opportunities to socialize and to have the extramarital affairs he justified to himself by the convenient excuse that his wife had become increasingly frigid.

Although outwardly they appeared happy, their easy way in the presence of others belied a disturbing ennui that threatened their marriage. Alone for extended periods, Helen found solace in the company of women, particularly at the YWCA where she swam and took evening courses. Symeon interpreted her antipathy to him as evidence she was seeing someone else. It mattered little that he himself was unfaithful. It mattered to him only that his wife remain true.

"Who is he?" he yelled at her one day. "Who are you seeing?"

"There is no one," she replied. "I neither want nor need another man."

After numerous attempts at rational discourse, they finally agreed that Helen should get away. But where to? Egypt was out of the question after King Farouk had abdicated his throne and most of the Barroses' friends had left the country. Alexandria, which for years had been home to people from every part of the Levant, was no longer the cosmopolitan city providing a distinct European flavor to the African continent.

Because of political unrest in both Egypt and Greece, neither country interested Helen, whose thoughts drifted back to earlier days and to people she once enjoyed. She wanted to travel to Wisconsin to see Lula. And although there had been an inexcusable lapse in their correspondence, Helen knew she would be well received.

———

With one suitcase in hand and a few dollars in her purse, Helen boarded the Hiawatha in Chicago for the last leg of the trip to Eagle Creek. Two hours earlier she had stepped off the train from New York, dizzy from alcohol and lack of sleep. The all-day and overnight ride was spent largely in the bar car, for her Pullman offered little rest or reprieve from the jerky motion of the train. Settled at a window seat, she stared aimlessly at the backs of city streets until the welcoming farms of Wisconsin came into view. She dozed intermittently, getting up only to relieve herself, when at last she was startled by the conductor, who told her the next stop would be hers.

As she and one other person were helped off the train, it appeared to Helen as though a welcoming party had arrived to greet them both. She was not aware that meeting the train was a popular pastime for people in that small town. And like the telephone office, where the Lundgren sisters listened vicariously to other people's conversations while manning the switchboard, so, too, was the train station part of the town's information-gathering and dispersal system. When the comings and goings at the depot had been duly noted by those assembled, everyone departed as the Hiawatha pulled away.

"There's no taxi in these parts," the man said. "Lincoln Avenue is three blocks down Main Street and one to the left. The Sarris house is on the right at the corner."

Helen picked up her bag and began walking.

———

As she entered the room, Helen fell into Lula's arms, and for the longest time neither uttered a word. The silence was broken when she whispered, "Lula, how wonderful you look. My God, look at you. No longer the child I remember. You're a woman now—and your breasts!" Wiping her eye with a finger, she stood at arm's length holding Lula's hand and asked, "Are you happy? Has life been good?"

"I'm happy," Lula replied. "Sometimes lonely, but I'm happy. You look well too—different maybe, but still the same Helen I remember." Nervously she continued, "How are you? Where are your valises?"

She drew herself towards Helen, whose hand she still held—happy that the days ahead would allow them to reminisce and become reacquainted. But Helen did look different. Her hair was short, cut like a boy's. And she was wearing pants, something Lula's husband believed women should never do. The lines of her once elegantly attired body were now obscured by disheveled clothes. Perhaps it was from traveling, Lula thought, as she looked closer at her friend. Disturbing, however, was the unmistakable odor of tobacco on Helen's clothing.

When she saw the candied sweets and pastry laid out for her, Helen said, "Lula, you shouldn't have bothered. We aren't in Greece now, and nobody will question your hospitality—certainly not me. Do you have whiskey? I'd like some whiskey if you have any. I know it's early, but it will relax me after the long train ride. It took over eight hours to come just from Chicago alone."

"No whiskey—only the Metaxa we keep for company. Will that be all right?"

"For now, yes."

Lula returned from the kitchen holding the long slender bottle of the Greek brandy with the same name as the prime minister of Greece who said no to the Axis forces at the onset of World War II. Powerful as the verbal rejection was of Mussolini in the winter of 1940 is the drink itself, which Lula sometimes nipped to ease an occasional cough. She had no sooner filled the bottom of a tumbler when Helen remarked, "Lula, I'm a grown woman. Please dear, fill the glass."

They talked. They laughed, tearfully at times, recalling moments from the past. Lula spoke proudly of her children and their grandmother's efforts to teach them Greek. She recalled how during their voyage to America, Helen had been her teacher as well. She said Christos was a good husband who, although distant at times, knew what his responsibilities were. She had no complaints about her life and was saddened to learn of the difficulties Helen and Symeon were having. But when Helen asked for more Metaxa, Lula quietly but firmly told her it was time for her to lie down.

"We have days to talk. Now you should rest. Come, let me take you to your room."

Lula covered her guest with one of Stamatia's afghans and drew the shades.

"Let me kiss you, my darling," Helen said reaching for Lula's hand. "I'm glad I came."

———

Helen remained in Eagle Creek three weeks. Her presence brought back memories for Christos and Lula of the time spent together in Athens and Paris and of the heady days crossing the Atlantic. They were pleased she had come to renew an old friendship, now rekindled as they spoke of their lives in America. They recalled first impressions of each other and noted how everyone had changed since then.

As gratifying as it was to be reunited with their guest, however, Christos and Lula felt a certain uneasiness in her presence as the visit progressed. They observed that Helen, when given the opportunity, could remain in bed the entire day, and while up and about hardly seemed the vibrant woman they remembered her to have been. They were concerned that she had come alone and seldom mentioned her husband, who once was Christos's best friend. And although Helen alluded to difficulties in her marriage, the troubled nature of her personal life was not fully appreciated by her hosts, nor the compounding effect alcohol was having on it.

"Come! It's a beautiful day and I want to pick *horta*," Lula called out one morning, holding a straw basket and two small knives. "Bring along your sweater. It's chilly outside."

Helen followed obediently, wondering what was in store, for she knew Lula was attempting to engage her in something that might lift her spirits. As they walked along the street to the edge of town, it immediately became apparent what had been programmed. Lula stopped at the first sight of a dandelion, stooped down, and deftly extracted the plant with one of the instruments she carried.

"See those two over there? Get them for me," she directed, motioning to Helen. "Here, use this other knife. The townspeople thought we were crazy when they first saw us gathering dandelion greens. They didn't know they could be eaten. Well, we know they can. Would you believe we even had to tell our grocer to carry garlic, olive oil, and oregano for us?"

Helen was amused by what was happening. Never before involved in anything resembling farming, she was hesitant at first to dig. In no time, however, she was scouring the area for the freshest-looking greens. The hunt for *horta* had indeed elevated her mood, and she appeared energized by the experience. There they were, two friends on a morning's mission to pull from the earth some of its abundant offerings.

They gathered enough for their evening meal and were returning when Helen spoke: "Lula, your husband loves you. Everyone loves you. You came for a better life and found it in this wilderness with a man wanting a family. And you have your mother, too. With Symeon and me, it's different. He wants no children and I am alone. I have no family. Maybe our problem is me. My husband is the same man he has always been. No different from before. But I know I have changed. I am a different person now."

Lula was perplexed. "Different, how?" she asked.

Helen hesitated, and only after an uncomfortable silence replied, "Lula, you won't understand even if I try to explain."

Lula responded that no one was without problems and that, for many people, life becomes more difficult with time and for different reasons. Confused by what Helen was saying, Lula chose not to pursue the issue further, and instead quietly took her friend's hand as they walked along the river toward home.

"Go back to Symeon. Talk to him about your feelings, if you can. There should be nobody else in your lives for either of you."

It was an awkward moment for both women. Lula was saying one thing while Helen was thinking another.

"A man cannot pretend with a woman, like a woman can with a man," was Helen's response. "I drink to forget that my life is other than it seems."

Helen believed Lula had failed to comprehend her dilemma, yet Lula now understood what was being alluded to.

"I see the pain on your face and know there is more in your heart," Lula said. "I would help you, Helen, if I could. Speak to your priest when you are home. What better advice can I give you?"

"You can't, my dear Lula. *Inshallah*. Years ago I wanted to make you into a lady. More than that now, you have become a woman, a real one, not one like me."

Lula made no effort to avoid the hand that was extended to her as they slowly walked home, carrying with them the greens they had gathered.

On arrival, they emptied the basket on the kitchen table, shaking sand off the leaves before washing them. Helen asked if she could be of help in the kitchen, but was reminded that duties of the hearth were within the purview of a hostess.

"Go lie down and get some rest. I'll call if I need you. Better still, phone your husband—something I don't believe you've done yet. He should know how you are and when to expect you back."

"I have an idea," Helen said. "Let me make supper. I'm feeling better and I want to do something useful."

Surprised by the suggestion, Lula smiled and agreed. "Do you have anything in mind to make?"

"I can boil the greens. We have olives and the cheese that came yesterday from Chicago. Oh, I know—I'll make my lentil soup. It's special. And with the bread your mother baked this morning, we won't need anything more, except maybe fruit, which we have. And wine, of course."

Relinquishing her role as the *chef de maison*, Lula smiled. Amazed by her guest's burst of enthusiasm, she said, "Tell me, Helen, what makes your soup special? What secret ingredients will you need?"

"I put in equal parts of water to either beef or chicken broth. Then

I mix some yellow peas with the lentils. And at the end, I season with cinnamon. All of this I learned from our Egyptian cook, who reminded me that cinnamon comes from trees and was used as medicine in ancient times to make people happy. Isn't that why we Greeks sprinkle cinnamon on so many things for happy occasions—especially with honey? I think so."

After laying out everything she believed would be needed, Lula departed, returning at intervals to note Helen's progress and to set the table. Peering through the kitchen door, Stamatia shook her head and said nothing.

The meal was a success. The lentil soup met everyone's expectations as Helen and Lula smiled at each other from opposite ends of the table. Stamatia, who was praised for her bread sat quietly eating as the others spoke. After two glasses of wine, Christos imagined himself in the Peloponnese.

Helen remained in Eagle Creek several more days, during which she refrained from smoking in the presence of her hosts, although they knew from the odor of her clothes that she had regularly done so. She drank wine only at meals and suppressed overt signs of affection until it was time for her to depart.

At the train station, Helen thanked her hosts for their hospitality and asked if she could visit again. As they embraced, she whispered in Lula's ear that she loved her. To Christos standing nearby she said, "Take good care of our lady until we see each other again."

She waved through the window as the train pulled away.

10. Family Album

"Life is short, opportunity fleeting, experiment treacherous, judgment difficult." —*Hippocrates*

A HOSPITAL IS MORE THAN A PLACE OF SOLACE AND HEALING. For many it is where a need to nurture can be expressed. For others it is a venue where experiences are shared and memories are made. For Martha Ravitch and Daisy Butler, it was a point where their dissimilar lives intersected during a medical emergency and developed into a relationship beyond the confines of the hospital itself. Grateful for the treatment her son had received at Hamilton General and particularly appreciative of its nursing staff, Daisy was determined to continue the efforts begun under supervision. It was acceptable and convenient, she believed, that her other children were looked after by their aunt.

"This child be special," she thought as she went about caring for Tyrone. Her cousin could be responsible for the girls. The boy was Daisy's to fuss over. "He pull on the nipples like he tear me apart. Even when I know he eaten good, he cry and cry when I takes him off and burp him. And when I put him back in his crib, he still cry. It ain't the colic—oh, he just an ornery one. He mad all the time, need to have his way. Jesus, don't let him be mean and nasty like his father when he grow up. Anyway, he make the girls happy. Look at his pecker."

The first two years of Tyrone's life were beset by the usual childhood ailments. Occasional diarrhea with bouts of vomiting, painful teething, and the first high fever were taken in stride by a mother whose commitment to her son was fierce. And during that time, the boy steadily grew and was found to be within normal parameters of growth for his age. But the moment had arrived for Daisy to return to housekeeping for her clients. She looked forward to renewing an acquaintance with Martha Ravitch, who on return from Nicaragua was overwhelmed by her own responsibilities.

Daisy called Martha, offering the help that had once been promised. And what began as a weekly housekeeping visitation evolved into a daily all-purpose display of assistance that grew into a friendship as well. In short order, Martha felt confident assigning the care of her son to Daisy before leaving for the hospital each morning; Daisy in return happily earned money doing things she hardly thought of as work. Occasionally, she brought along her son for Martha to see and compare with her own, during which times the din of children's cries and adult voices permeated the Ravitch apartment. And so it began. Weeks turned into months and months became years. All the while, Martha and Daisy committed to one another and to each other's child.

———

Although he was the adopted son of a single Jewish parent, it was clear that Evan Ravitch was also a mestizo, the term used in Central and South America to describe a person of mixed Spanish and Indian blood. He was a handsome youth with high cheekbones and glistening black hair. His copper skin color defined his lineage. When strangers saw him with his mother, they seemed perplexed as to his origin, fantasizing, no doubt, that some exotic assignation had produced such a striking youth. Knowing glances were more apparent whenever Dr. Sarris accompanied mother and son to a restaurant or the cinema, as he often did.

Tyrone Butler was a black American. The same age as Evan, he stood four inches taller, and over the years had developed into a larger and more athletic youth. Active in sports, Tyrone was forever kicking a soccer ball or engaging someone in a game of catch, his baseball mitt always at the ready. His teachers labeled him hyperkinetic, but Martha assured his mother he was only, as she put it, "adrenaline-charged," and that this physiologic characteristic would one day serve him well in competitive sports. It was, she said, the fight-flight response that was part of his genetic makeup. Nothing to worry about.

In spite of their differences, the boys got along well whenever Daisy brought her son to the Ravitch home, and over time they became friends. As youngsters, Evan excelled in any intellectual duel, and Tyrone sported his physical superiority when the need to impress or control presented itself. As they played together, each understood the other's advantage and guarded his own space. They were thirteen years old, going on fourteen.

As the boys' friendship grew, so did their mothers'. To Martha, Daisy was more than a cleaning lady and a reliable babysitter. Rather, she was a person eager to learn from those about her, and by so doing had gained access to a world she would have otherwise never known. Quietly going about her chores, she often fantasized about a far-off future caring for patients on some hospital ward and being involved in their lives. When Martha brought home accounts of the day's happenings, Daisy listened and later relived each event in her mind exactly as portrayed.

In the years their friendship endured, the women thought of themselves as sisters sharing intimate details of their lives. Martha not only needed Daisy's help in maintaining an orderly home, but also worried about her friend's financial health, providing extra money when she could. Daisy was concerned that Martha's personal world seemed constricted and wondered where the relationship with Dr. Leo was headed, now that they had decided to become roommates. She was determined one day to find out after coming across a note on the kitchen table that proved to be a poem Martha had once written:

Rooms swept clean, furniture spaced
To fit that pattern which seems appropriate.
Rugs vacuumed, tuft high,
While windows sparkle
Like prisms deflecting rainbow rays.
Not a dust particle lingers unnecessarily.
Once again I am ready, but will he come?
Or will this day pass like others
With hard work spent
Just in case?

———

"How many years you be with Dr. Leo?" Daisy asked.

"How old are the boys?" Martha countered. "Almost fifteen years, I guess, and I don't know what I would have done without him."

Daisy had never questioned any living arrangement that existed between her friends. She herself once had a common-law husband. But the domestic situation of Martha and Leo sharing an apartment seemed to her out of the ordinary for white folks.

"I know you be married before," Daisy continued.

"Twice before. Remember? But you know that, so why are you talking about it now?"

"Because I see you unhappy these days. Maybe cuz you not married?"

"Not unhappy, Daisy, and not because I'm not married. Just a little concerned now that Evan is getting older. He's grown a lot in the last few months. You see his little mustache, don't you? He's getting sassy and his voice cracks when he's excited. You know what that means."

"Yup—trouble. Just like my Tyrone. I see that stick pokin' out under his pants all the time. They ain't little boys no more."

Martha untangled the load of clothes just out of the dryer, folding some items and giving others to Daisy before going on.

"When Dr. Leo said he would help me become a mother, he knew I would need him for support and to be sort of a husband—not a real husband tied down with problems of money and all that, but like a partner sharing things. So, we give and take as much as we can, stay apart when we want, and come together when it's important."

"I know," Daisy replied. "Like when you was sick and when your boy had his appendix out. He worry for you like a good man do. We worry together, and he make me come stay in your house them days. Remember? So, girl, why you sad?"

"I'm not sad. I told you that," Martha replied. "But Leo said something that bothers me now that Evan needs a man like Leo in his life. They argued over some little thing and Evan hollered at Leo, saying he wasn't his father and that he couldn't tell him what to do anymore. 'Just my mother's boyfriend,' he said. 'That's all you are, so leave me alone.' "

"Don't be upset, Miss Martha. The boy be jealous of the doctor. He wants you all for hisself. He know he ain't got no real daddy, no brothers and sisters, no cousins, and he not old enough to understand his mama have enough love for both her men. But you got to let him know he the most important person to you, but the doctor be important too. You hear?"

Martha did worry there could be problems ahead; she saw that Evan's attitude towards his "father" had unsettled Leo. She wondered if the new "adult-youth" dynamic that had developed between the two males would in any way affect everyone's feelings. Until then, Martha never seriously considered the question. Aware of Leo's constant interaction at work with faces younger and prettier than hers, however, she now had even greater cause than she sometimes had in the past to ponder his commitment to her and her son in the extent of obvious rejection.

As far as their relationship was concerned, it had never been a matter of philosophy or religion that stood in the way of a possible marriage, as their views on most issues, although different in many ways, were for the most part reconcilable. Martha had always wanted children and now had a son in her life. Leo did not feel the world was owed his mirror image and was not obsessed by a need to see himself replicated. The desire to provide his parents with the grandchildren they coveted was not reason enough for him to marry, and to please them with a suitable daughter-in-law would surely have meant that Martha was not the right choice.

How to worship God was another matter. Believing strongly that his Christianity represented the fulfillment of Martha's Judaism, Leo derived pleasure from their frequent discussions on the theological and historical relationship of one faith to the other without attempting to judge the spirituality inherent in either. As to practice, he was comfortable living his faith as best he could, while Martha was less assertive in the manner she expressed her beliefs. Consequently, Evan often felt confusion and ambiguity about religion, as he came to know only cultural elements of both without understanding the fundamental tenets of either.

Leo Sarris was an enigma to many at Hamilton General Hospital. Talented in his work, he was regularly requested for difficult cases, in spite of his reputation for being "difficult" in the operating room. Frivolity in his presence was not tolerated; the practice of medicine to him was serious business. His personal goal had always been to be the best he could be, and he meant it when he said, "A bad surgeon needs a good anesthesiologist; a good surgeon deserves one." Yet, the hospital was only a part of his world. At the end of the day, he chose, more often than not, to be alone.

Leo's idea of an evening well spent included the opportunity to read or listen to music, and scattered about the apartment was evidence of that fact. Books, recordings, magazines, medical journals, and newspapers could be found everywhere. Although his interest in classical music had taken him on a trip from the baroque to the modernists of the twentieth century, it was the religiosity he felt when listening to Bruckner and the pathos expressed in the complexities of a Mahler score that best held his interest.

It disturbed Leo to have music in the background as he read, and conversely, when absorbed in his music, he permitted no other activity. It was an either-or issue, except during moments of meditation. From the monks on Mount Athos he had learned to experience the serenity that comes with quiet repetitions of the Jesus prayer: "Lord Jesus Christ, Son of God, have mercy on me, a sinner."

Dr. Sarris was a believer. There had to be a higher being, a force, a God, if you will, who had put the world together. Taught by his mother to pray, he sought "divine assistance" during moments of stress, and it didn't seem paradoxical to him as a physician to do so. He prayed every day on his way to the hospital that he would, as he had pledged when taking the Hippocratic oath, to do no harm. He understood that in his work he was juxtaposed between good and evil, and life and death as God's right-hand helper.

Consumed by his career, Leo saw no need for change. He knew his personal life was complicated, but it was acceptable to him as it stood. He was a partner in a stable relationship that offered him the freedom to be the loner he had always thought himself as being. It was Martha who increasingly sensed an anxiety that was difficult to explain. Was it her son's pubescence or questions she harbored of an uncertain future with Leo that were surfacing with increasing regularity?

———

Hearing music one evening, Martha knew Leo was relaxing and probably in good spirits. As was his habit, he had retired to his "space" after dinner to read and regroup from the day's activities. The ravishingly beautiful sound of stringed instruments prompted her to pause when she realized the same orchestral movement was being repeated.

"Can the good doctor be disturbed?" she asked as she entered the room. "What is that you're listening to?"

Leo answered it was the *Adagietto,* or slow movement, from Gustav Mahler's Fifth Symphony. Putting his book down, he made room on the sofa as he motioned for her to sit with him and listen.

"It's one of the most beautiful things ever composed, in my opinion. I had to hear it after reading some German tonight," he said. "In college we read several works of Thomas Mann and this particular story, *A Death in Venice* is the one I remember best. And that's why I thought of Mahler."

"Why? Is there some relationship between the music and what you're reading?" she asked.

"Yes, there is: both a historical and an intellectual connection between the author and the composer. Story has it that Mann was inspired to write *Death in Venice* after seeing Mahler break down in tears on a train departing Venice. I don't know the details of the encounter, but they did know each other and were both products of the same Central European culture. Interestingly enough, this beautiful score was repeatedly used in the soundtrack for Visconti's soporific film adaptation of the book."

When the music ended, Martha made a comment that pleased Leo when she remarked that the *Adagietto* was gratifyingly long enough to make its point.

"You're right, Martha, it really is. In fact, most all the slow movements of Mahler's symphonies are lengthy and sumptuously written, but this one is my favorite. You know, much of what he composed has connotations of death and the hereafter. If I could arrange it, I'd have a full orchestra at my funeral playing this very music. And if I were to make it beyond the pearly gates, I'd want to be ushered in by the awesome finale of his Third Symphony."

"So, then, who died in Venice and why? Come on, put your book away and get comfortable. I know you're dying to tell the story," Martha said. "No pun intended." She was right. Leo was in the mood to talk. "Move to the end of the sofa so I can lie down," he said. And in quick order his head was nestled in Martha's lap.

"Before I start, you should know that Mann was awarded the Nobel Prize for literature in the thirties, and his *Death in Venice* is thought by many to be one of the most beautiful books written in the twentieth century. Aside from appreciating his literary style, I like Thomas Mann because his German is easy enough for me to read. Basically, the story is about an aging author who goes to Venice in search of spiritual fulfillment. And that fulfillment, instead, leads to his doom."

"Heavy stuff," Martha said.

"It is. The author visits an Italian seaside resort, where his infatuation with a young boy and the pleasure of recognizing pure beauty cause him to extend his stay despite warnings of a cholera epidemic. The central figure is Professor von Aschenbach, who, once installed in a comfortable hotel, notices among the guests an almost unnaturally beautiful Polish boy, Tadzio."

"Stop right there," Martha interrupted. "If this is a story about some old pederast, I don't care to hear it. I'd rather just listen to more music."

"Easy! It's not about that at all. It's really a profound study of ideas, symbols, morality, and all kinds of other things one can read into the short but simple plot. Can I go on now?"

"Go ahead." she said reluctantly. "Finish what you've started."

"Well, the old professor is slowly obsessed by the boy's beauty, but never once speaks to the kid. He just looks and imagines that a relationship develops between them. The old man is married and apparently heterosexual, but the boy's beauty reawakens some dormant emotions and the old geezer is disturbed by the whole scene. Well, you can figure out the rest. Despite warnings of the epidemic, he stays in Venice, comes down with cholera, and dies."

"Does the boy ever show any interest in the old guy, or is everything happening only in the professor's mind?" Martha wanted to know. "And if they never speak, how is it possible to have a relationship with someone by sight alone? Or is it?"

"In the book, the boy glances only once at the old man and that's all the contact there is between them," Leo replied. "Can a relationship exist without conversation? I suppose in one's imagination it can. Personally, I'd want to speak with anyone I'm interested in. But I think the attraction is something other than sexual, that Tadzio represents more than that to the old man. The boy represents the pleasures of pure beauty. And the story points out how it's possible for one to sacrifice one's well-being to the immediate experience of that beauty. Does it make sense? Or is it all a bit far out for you?"

Martha took her time answering. "It's not that much to understand," she said. "It's a simple enough plot, I guess. If one views it as an allegory, one can read things into it that are straightforward enough. You tell me it's beautifully written in German, but I don't see myself rushing to buy a translation, now that I know what the story is about."

"Oh, you don't care for the plot because it involves a young boy and an old man. Am I right? Well, think beyond the plot and only of the ideas the story suggests," was Leo's response.

"Maybe so, but right now I'm thinking only of a hot tub and a glass of wine. How about you?"

Martha slowly extracted herself from the seat, pushing Leo's head aside as she got up to leave. He put his book away and reached for another recording, knowing it would be some time before it was his turn to shower. Returning to the sofa, he stretched out again, only now the music playing was from *Tristan and Isolde*.

A half hour later, Martha emerged from the bathroom, appearing in terry cloth from head to toe, a white towel covering her hair. Her robe, untied at the waist, exposed her naked body as she slid past Leo, whose turn it was to wash up.

"I'll open the bottle so the wine can breathe," she said.

"And remember to screw in the cork all the way," he laughed, recalling a previous episode.

It was not possible for Martha to hide her intent from Leo, who easily read her coded signals. The look she gave as she glided past him on her way to the kitchen and the lingering graze against his thigh told him what he needed to know. His toilet would be brief—a shower, mouthwash, and dabs of cologne at strategic points, a routine he had learned from her.

"Cheers," they said taking their first sips, and then more wine and still more, as if attempting to hurry the moment. *Kefi* it was called in Turkish, a word denoting the state of being in the mood or getting "turned on."

The soaring notes of Wagner's music, the glow brought on by the grape, and the warmth of each other's touch as they sat listening to the love duet from that famous opera had brought them to their *kefi*.

"Leo, will you feel my breast and see if I have a lump here?" she asked.

For a moment he believed she was serious, but after examining the spot she had pointed to, he smiled, knowing it was but a signal for him to begin. He took her breast in both hands and gently fondled it, making sure he brushed her nipple all the while. And when it was firmly erect, he put his lips to it, moving his tongue back and forth while biting it, oh so gently. He heard her muffled sigh as she attempted to speak his name. Beginning slowly at first and with gradual acceleration, he massaged her body and then her thighs and finally her pudendum until he knew the moment was right. Carrying her into the bedroom, he pulled off her robe and then his own, without letting his lips leave hers as they began making love. He knew what pleased her, as did she in return.

They were in each other's arms an hour later. The lights were on and the music had stopped. Martha slowly wiggled herself free, massaging an arm that had fallen asleep under his body. She showered and returned, taking her place in bed beside him.

"On a scale of ten, for me this was an eleven," she said. "I had forgotten how good we could be together. It's been awhile."

"We've talked about that before. Let's not go there again."

"I know our schedules are wicked. But when you want to be—oh well, just tell me there isn't some younger woman."

"Not that, Martha. But I wonder at times if you'd be better off with some other man."

"I'm not for anyone else, and you know it. We've been living together—how long now? You've got all it takes to please me. Look at tonight. There was chemistry, wasn't there?"

"There was," he agreed.

Martha Ravitch's emotional life had its highs and lows, and being physical with another person was a variable of that equation. Touching and holding went far toward keeping her emotions in check, but were in themselves no substitutes for sex. There were moments when she needed it all.

She was physically attractive and knew it. Not a beautiful woman, but striking in appearance and in the way she carried herself. Slender and sinewy, which made her seem taller than she was, especially on occasions when she wore high heels. But it was her raven black hair, graying at the temples, that caught one's attention, and her deeply set blue eyes bespoke of a probable liaison enjoyed by a distant ancestor. There was no doubt she was of Mediterranean stock.

Leo Sarris worried too much about his appearance, so Martha often told him. She chided him about the comb-over styling of his thinning hair and said, "God created but few perfect heads, and the rest he grew hair on." Leo lectured others on the significance of lean muscle mass and the need for dietary discipline. He worked out at the gym; he knew there were parts of his body he could control in terms of size and performance.

"What time is it now?" he asked.

"A few minutes past two," she replied.

"Oh God, set the alarm for six. I've got a big day tomorrow."

11. Boys

"Of all the animals, the boy is the most unmanageable."
—Plato

*H*ERE, TAKE ONE. THESE ARE STRONGER than the ones I got last week, so don't inhale too deep or they'll make you puke. Taste like medicine. Says there's menthol in 'em. Don't know why they put that shit in cigarettes. Maybe so they can call 'em Kools. Cool cigarettes. Get it?"

Holding the pack in his extended hand, Tyrone Butler offered a second cigarette to Evan, who let it dangle from the corner of his mouth, as he had seen in the movies. Tyrone pressed his own cigarette against Evan's, telling him to take a "drag."

"That's a Dutch fuck we've just had, you know?"

"What do you mean?" asked Evan, drawing puffs as they spoke. "What's a Dutch fuck?"

"Don't know how it got that name. That's what they call it when you get a light off 'a somebody else's cigarette. Got that from Hector— you know, the dude that gets me stuff. Says he can get booze, too, if I want."

Tyrone and Evan had met Hector Torres several times before at an empty garage where they smoked. There he proudly exhibited his collection of pornographic cards and introduced the boys to masturbation. An acquaintance of Tyrone's, Hector shared an apartment with his older brother in the building where Daisy Butler and her family lived. She was concerned about the frequent coming and going of visitors at the Torreses' place and repeatedly told her son to stay away.

Daisy worried about Tyrone's association with Hector, for she knew that as adolescents they were capable of unpredictable and loathsome behavior. She was unable to erase from her memory the picture of once having seen Hector heartlessly stabbing a stray cat, which Tyrone had wounded with his BB gun.

"Jeez, this stuff is strong," Evan said, beginning to cough. "I think I'm getting sick." He sat on the floor, his head slowly spinning as a rush of cold perspiration suddenly came over him. In a prelude to vomiting, he salivated profusely. Rumbling from his belly heralded the impending crisis. Then he threw up.

"Man, what's the matter with you? I told ya to go easy. And gimme that smoke before you set the joint on fire. I'll finish it. No use wastin' the stuff."

Tyrone had been held back a year in school and was now in the eighth grade. At one time, school officials believed he had a learning disability, when in fact it was his truancy that had kept him a year behind Evan. Although the boys were the same age, they differed in other ways. Tyrone was street smart, having grown up in a neighborhood where wit and guile were valued. Larger than Evan and pushy by nature, he appeared older than he was.

Not a stellar student, Evan, on the other hand, had made steady progress in school, and for his age was relatively poised and articulate, the influence of his mother and her circle of friends. Recently, however, he was looking more and more in the direction of Tyrone's world.

"Beer can get you sick, too, if you drink too much," Tyrone said. "But it makes a guy feel good. So, if you can cop some money off your ole lady, I'll get Hector to buy us a pack. Okay?"

Unsteady as he left the lair, Evan wasn't thinking of cigarettes or booze, but instead whether the smell of tobacco would betray him to his mother.

———

Years later, sitting in a courtroom, Daisy Butler fought hard to hold back tears as her son faced the judge about to sentence him for breaking and entering. With three prior counts of petty larceny on record, the magistrate concluded that Tyrone now had to serve time.

The sentence was a year to be spent at a center for juvenile offenders. He was seventeen.

"What did I do wrong?" Daisy repeatedly asked herself as she watched her son being taken away. "The best I could. Without a father and me workin' all day, he have nobody to make him behave. He be a problem to me, I knew the first day I laid eyes on him he be a problem. I hope he come out a better man than he go in. Lord have mercy."

It was wishful thinking for her to believe incarceration would prove to be of any therapeutic value in Tyrone's case. Yet, Daisy hoped that somehow the discipline she was unable to impose over the years would now be forced upon her son, who would then respond and emerge a better person—older, but with a sense of direction he had heretofore lacked.

But it was not to be, for as in any adult prison, the skills required of a person to cope with life in a juvenile facility were the same. In order to withstand bullying, one had to bully. To avoid being preyed upon, one became the aggressor, all the while feigning the image of a model inmate. Prison was a graduate school of sorts, an educational level superior to that of the city streets, where lessons were learned, courses were taught, and the arts of extortion, deception, and coercion were perfected with an eye to future use.

When Tyrone came home to live again with his mother, Daisy believed she saw a difference in him from when he had left. He had gained weight and appeared taller. Quieter than before and somewhat subdued in demeanor, Tyrone was content to remain at home most of the day, watching television and responding grudgingly to his mother's exhortations to look for work. But the minimum-wage opportunities available to people with a prison record held little appeal to him, and he continued to languish while his mother worked all day.

"Get out the house. Do something," she screamed one morning as she was about to leave. "Go work. You a man now. You big and strong enough. Help me put food on the table."

"There has to be a better way," Tyrone thought to himself. "I need money, yeah, but bagging groceries ain't for me."

Hesitating at first, he picked up the phone and called his old friend and neighbor, Hector Torres.

"He don't live here anymore. Has his own place now," his mother replied when she gave out his number.

———

Martha Ravitch knew creating a life for her son would not be easy, and it was her good fortune that many people assisted her during Evan's early years. Considered somewhat of an oddity by some of the hospital family, Evan garnered affection from unexpected sources, especially from Martha's colleagues on the nursing staff. But it was from Daisy Butler, the preferred caregiver in his mother's absence, that he received the most attention. Looking after him was a "piece of chocolate cake", as she put it, compared to the difficulties she encountered with Tyrone.

As Evan grew older, Martha sometimes questioned her own performance as a single parent, causing her to wonder whether in her haste to have a family she had acted wisely in her choice of adoption. Were she to have had a daughter instead of a son, might she have been better prepared addressing girl things? Was she overly concerned about the possibility of her son becoming a sissy from the influences of so many women in his life?

She felt guilty whenever those or other thoughts crossed her mind. She loved her son just as he was and couldn't imagine a life without him. For advice on boyhood issues, she turned most often to Jim Sarris as her son grew older.

"Stop beating up on yourself, Martha. Don't second-guess yourself. You've done a hell of a good job with Evan, something not many others would have ever attempted." Leo told her.

"No, we've all pitched in. You, Daisy, me. I guess I'm lucky there was something worthwhile there to begin with," Martha replied.

———

Evan Ravitch broke no academic record in high school and was scheduled to graduate with his class—a feat in no small part abetted by the constant nagging of his mother and Dr. Sarris. What began early in his teens as a testy relationship with his surrogate father gradually diminished as Evan eventually understood that the endless insistence for him to work hard would not abate.

"You're a good kid, so make something out of yourself. Think of what it would be like if you were living now in Nicaragua," the doctor said. "And look where you'd be if you were still hanging out with your friend Tyrone."

Over time Evan recognized he had been given a unique opportunity in life and that his comfortable middle-class existence was the gift of a selfless woman whose happiness was tied to his. But he also knew he was perceived by friends to be different. And at home he had no real father.

To his credit, he distanced himself from Tyrone Butler, who on several occasions had been expelled from school and was placed a second time in a detention center for threatening a teacher with a knife. Evan had come to realize that hanging out with him was a prelude to trouble. He knew, as did Martha and Daisy, that Tyrone was a disturbed youth, one who didn't care that he was estranged from virtually every person who knew him.

Dr. Leo supported Evan during his adolescent years by showing an interest in his studies and extracurricular activities. Not large in stature, Evan was a fast runner, an ability that earned him a place on the soccer team, where size mattered little. He played the trumpet in the school band and joined others in an effort to form a jazz group.

Girls, however, were another matter. Although he was comfortable in their presence and rarely missed a school dance, he never spoke of having a steady girlfriend. Perhaps it was an awareness that his darker skin set him apart from the blond girls he preferred. Perhaps it was insecurity that caused him to hold them at arm's length. Or was it the endless maternal warnings about sexually transmitted diseases that were more compelling than any instruction he may have received in basic sex education?

"I want to join the Marines," he confided one day to Leo. "I want to find out what's out there and get away from my mother and all of the other mothers I've had all my life. I know Mom can afford sending me to college, but I don't know if I'm college material. I think the service will help me decide a lot of things. Will you talk to her for me? I think she wants me around, but with you here she won't be alone."

Not letting on that he was pleased with the boy's decision Dr. Sarris agreed, for he understood Evan's need for self-validation. Leo himself had once thought of suggesting the military option to him when he finished high school.

"It's a great idea," he replied. "I'll speak to Martha."

A week before graduation, Evan appeared at the recruiting office and a month later was on his way to boot camp in North Carolina. At the bus station he kissed his mother good-bye.

"No tears, Mom. I'll be okay," he said.

"*Semper fidelis,*" Dr. Sarris called out when Evan stepped onto the bus.

12. Transition

*"O sleep, O gentle sleep,
Nature's soft nurse! how have I
frightened thee."*

—Shakespeare

SOON AFTER EVAN LEFT HOME, LEO AND MARTHA decided to buy a house, which they did.

"It has to be big enough so we can keep our distance, yet small enough to allow us to be close if we want," said Leo. "I can't be bumping into someone every time I turn around. I need my space."

"You can have your space as long as I have mine. Maybe we can communicate by walkie-talkie." She knew that "space" was important to him.

They found a house, which included an attached "mother-in-law" apartment that could provide Sarris the sanctuary he wanted. It would be his place, a venue to accommodate his moods and requisite private moments. They shared a bed and took most meals together as their schedules permitted. Daisy Butler came once a week to clean.

Late one afternoon Leo Sarris retreated to his den, settling into a leather chair with his feet on an ottoman as he recalled the salient features of a procedure that had occupied him the greater part of a day. Although the expenditure of physical energy during that long and difficult case was not great, the emotional drain he experienced was another matter. He was exhausted, and fell asleep.

But he slept fretfully, and in less than an hour was awake, aware of perspiration that had seeped through his scrub suit and onto the chair. It was that dream again, the bright yellow vision that placed him in an underwater cave. As always, he could detect a light shining through the water above. But how could he reach the surface to the source of illumination? As before, he would awaken before any resolution had occurred. Only this time it was different. In the dream, his mother was calling.

"You haven't heard from her in a long time and it wouldn't hurt to give her a ring," Martha said after speaking with Leo. "Call her now. I can see you're troubled. You'll feel better if you do."

Whether by extrasensory perception, telepathy, or some other form of cosmic transmission, Leo Sarris knew he had communicated at times with his mother in extraordinary ways. And as the scientist he believed he was, he tried to discount notions of a superhuman intelligence.

Yet, he remembered instances of nonverbal contact he had experienced before, on one occasion when he was having an operation on his foot. Upon calling home that evening to inform his parents that he had undergone a surgical procedure, his father told him that at the exact moment he was being wheeled into the operating room, his mother woke up, sat upright in bed, and stated there was a problem with her son. And at other times, she seemed able to fathom his thoughts from afar, as he was able to sense hers. Was she trying to contact him now? He picked up the phone and called.

"I'm afraid," she said. "I'm afraid of everything, that something terrible is going to happen." Speaking rapidly, his mother continued, "And I don't know why I'm so tired, I can't seem to move. I fall asleep at night and wake up two hours later, wide-awake staring at the ceiling. I can't eat. Ever since your grandmother died, I worry about death and other terrible things that could harm all of us."

It was not the mother Leo Sarris was accustomed to hearing. Ordinarily, she spoke in measured phrases and in a confident and assured way. Now there was agitation and fear in her voice. She began to cry.

"Is Dad there with you? Let me talk to him."

From his father, Leo learned that since Stamatia's death, Lula had become despondent, a condition thought to be normal under the circumstances and one that would improve with time. Lula had been seen by several doctors, who couldn't determine any physical illness. Rather, they said she was "melancholic" and would slowly get well. Patience was the only advice given Christos. Not wanting to leave his wife alone and unattended, he sought a person to care for her in his absence. Through a Greek-American newspaper he found a woman able to come to Eagle Creek and live in.

Her mother's sudden death was difficult for Lula to accept. Stoic throughout her life, Stamatia appeared to have been well and complained only of headaches made worse by cheese and wine. Arrangements had been made for her to see old Dr. Baker, but she was reluctant to go. She died in her sleep one day following a canceled appointment.

The two women had been companion and confidante to each other. Having firmly planted roots in American soil, they created for themselves a semblance of Greece in their new world. Wherever Lula now turned, she saw reflections of her mother, from the crocheted doilies on the sofa to the icon corner in the living room—all reminders of their lives together.

As a dutiful, loving and respectful daughter, she honored Stamatia's wishes that when the Lord called her home, she be dressed in blue and laid out in a blue-and-white-trimmed casket, the colors of the Greek flag. Most important, she had asked that two young priests with good voices be found to conduct her funeral. Stamatia knew the open- casket event would be a first to be witnessed in Eagle Creek and wanted the service with its chanting and solemnity to illustrate the richness of her Orthodox faith. Everything took place as was ordered.

Lula's condition worsened soon after her mother's burial; a severe case of influenza that followed had deepened her depression. That, too, would be self-limited, the doctors said, and would slowly improve. But it hadn't. The live-in companion was convinced that Lula had been afflicted by the evil eye and wondered whether an exorcism should be conducted.

"Get on a plane, Dad, and come here for another opinion and some help," Leo instructed his father. "Bring Mother as soon as you can."

At the airport, Dr. Sarris hardly recognized his mother when she entered the arrival area. He was struck by her drawn, expressionless face and her downward gaze. Gone was the effusive greeting he had been accustomed to receiving after periods away from home. Attempting a weak smile, she apologized for the problem she was causing, whispering that she was embarrassed.

"Mother," Leo said, "you're here now. I want you with me. Everything will be all right, you'll see."

He placed an arm around her shoulder as they walked to the car, offering assurances as they drove away. Arrangements had been made to go directly to the office of a psychiatrist who in Leo's opinion was not big on Freudian analysis but was known instead for the aggressive type of therapy he believed his mother needed. Dr. Johnson had agreed to see Lula as his last patient of the day to allow time for a good evaluation.

After two hours, Lula emerged from the interview and was directed by the doctor to an empty chair in the waiting room. Leo was asked to follow him into his office.

"Your mother is indeed severely depressed, but I am confident we can help her," Dr. Johnson began. "As you know, of all the psychiatric disorders we deal with, acute depression responds best to treatment. Although very sad and sometimes fearful and agitated, your mother is aware that something is wrong and that she is in need of help. That's a good sign. She worried she might be going crazy, as she put it, but was willing to talk, to explain her feelings as best she could. At times she cried, but she answered my questions and finally opened up, often in a torrent of words speaking about herself. She told me about her childhood in Greece and about moments of sadness experienced in her youth—how she felt, for example, when her pet lamb, which she knew by name, was slaughtered one Easter, and how she was not able to eat the flesh of the only playmate she had as a child.

"She talked at length about her marriage to a virtual stranger and about coming to this country, to a cold place, where she had no family except the single parent to whom she was anchored. She mentioned her boys and how much they meant to her and how lonely she became as each left home seeking a life of his own. She is a wise woman, I believe, with great understanding and is perhaps too sensitive not to have been affected by some of the difficult events of her life. And then her mother's death and the severe influenza that followed. Although the seeds of depression have probably always been within her, it was primarily her mother's passing, I suspect, that triggered the present situation. But we can help her."

"How?" Leo asked anxiously. "Will she be admitted to the hospital?"

"No, not at this time," Dr. Johnson replied. "Electroconvulsive therapy is what I would have turned to a few years ago, but now we save that as a last resort. Here's my plan. Today, many patients respond to one of the new antidepressant drugs available. I'd like to try some hefty doses of the tricyclic class to see what results we get. If that doesn't help, we can bring her into the hospital and begin a series of shock treatments. I want to avoid that if possible."

Relieved by what he was hearing, Leo said, "I don't know much about those medicines or how they work; I assume they're safe. If not in the hospital, where will she be treated?" he asked.

"With no underlying serious medical problem, your mother, in my opinion, can be treated at home if someone is always with her. I'm optimistic that drug therapy will work in her case, because she alluded to others in her family—her mother and an aunt— who also suffered from what were probably depressive disorders.

"People with a family history of depression often respond to medication alone. We know that in those individuals there is a predisposing genetic basis for the problem that exists, and given that susceptibility, a depression is sometimes triggered by an emotional or physical event. In your mother's case, she experienced both.

"The theory behind the mode of action of tricyclic drugs is that they inhibit the breakdown of neurotransmitter substance in the brain, in this case nor-epinephrine, thereby enhancing the performance of brain cells, particularly those of the cerebral cortex. It's certainly worth trying before resorting to more aggressive therapy."

As they spoke, Dr. Sarris's own spirits improved, for in the past few days he felt the weight of his mother's condition bearing down on him. Recalling the psychiatrist's words, he wondered if he, too, was genetically encoded to one day suffer a similar depression. Dismissing the idea, his concern now was for his mother, whose therapy would begin in the morning.

———

Leo and Martha took time off from work to administer the medicine prescribed by Dr. Johnson. After the first dose, Lula became sleepy, as her doctor said she would. When she grew unsteady and complained of dizziness, Martha led her to the bedroom, where she was undressed and put to bed.

"I know you're tired, Mrs. Sarris, so get some sleep. Leo and I will both be here with you when you wake up."

As the medicine began to work, Lula descended into a deep sleep, breathing heavily and scarcely changing positions. At regular intervals and with help, she was awakened and given more pills to take. So it went during the first day of therapy, as Lula was repeatedly medicated and allowed to sleep. On the second day she appeared less drowsy, but was kept in bed except to go to the toilet with help and to eat. On the third day, as the therapeutic regimen continued, Lula woke up early in the morning and was dressing herself when Martha came into the room.

"Here, let me comb your hair, Mrs. Sarris. Did you sleep well last night?"

"I feel better today, not so shaky inside. But I'm thirsty. Could I have some water, please, and maybe coffee, too?"

"I'll have both for you in minute."

Gradually, Lula's depression began to lift, and within days it was evident that the medication was working. She appeared more alert, began to comment on her surroundings, and was eager to converse with Martha, who before then she had hardly known.

Their conversations began with small talk, but as the women relaxed in each other's presence, their discussions took on a different dimension. They found themselves asking probing and substantive questions. Martha learned of the fears and anxieties Lula experienced when she came to the United States; Lula in turn heard for the first time of the mixed joy and insecurity shared by adoptive children and their parents. Little by little, old perceptions of each other were cast aside and new ones emerged as the women spoke of their lives. And the common denominator that prevailed during much of their discourse was Leo Sarris.

Lula's rapid recovery from what was initially a state of deep melancholy amazed everyone. The protocol prescribed by Dr. Johnson averted the need for more aggressive treatment, allowing Lula to return to Eagle Creek just over a month after she had left. Stabilized on a maintenance dose of medication, she appeared to be her old self again.

"I can't thank you enough for what you've done for me," Lula told Martha before departing. "You helped me, not only because of who I am, but also because I believe it is in your nature to care about others. If you love my son, you should marry him."

"Take care of yourself, Mrs. Sarris. We're both here if you need us. And try to forget how you felt before you came. Remember, Leo loves you very much—maybe more than anyone else, certainly more than me."

Holding Martha's hand as they walked to the gate, Lula said, "Don't wait to marry until a time when you think everything is perfect. That day might never come. Take a chance. I did, and I'm not sorry."

When a voice overhead was heard announcing the departure, Lula embraced her son and whispered, "She's a good person. Do something."

———

The two most important women in Leo Sarris's life had come together under difficult circumstances and become friends. Lula was comfortable in Martha's company and wondered why her son hadn't married the person who for a long time had been an important part of his life. Martha was drawn to a woman who represented the birth mother she never knew. The accented speech and Old World mannerisms completed an image of the person she imagined her mother to have been. Why, wondered Lula, hadn't her son made an effort before to present Martha to his parents? It couldn't have been approval he was concerned about, for surely he knew them better than to believe they would deny him their blessing.

In fairness to Leo, it was Martha who had early on determined the nature of their relationship. Convinced that another marriage was not in her or Evan's best interest, she felt no compelling need to alter the dynamic of their arrangement. She had, after all, a man who offered intimacy, social access, and the perception of stability.

Once home, Lula heard regularly from Dr. Johnson, who called during the evening when he knew she could be reached. Pleased with her progress, he regulated downward the dosage of her medication. He also inquired of her personal life, and was glad to learn she understood the importance of establishing relationships outside the home. To escape the confines of an empty house, she turned to the Sisters of the Sacred Heart, whom she assisted at the hospital and occasionally joined in evening prayer. She enjoyed a certain comfort level in their presence, recalling how, as a child, she herself had once thought of entering a convent.

Caring for Lula exposed Martha to an area of nursing she knew little about, for unlike her field of critical care in which therapeutic goals are clear, the subtle needs of a grieving psyche encountered in psychiatric patients are more difficult to assess. And by so doing, she was reminded that a person's pain did not always call for narcotics, and that the prescription of a warm embrace was not measured in milligrams. But most important, she was glad to have been able to contribute to Lula's recovery and for the opportunity that was provided to better know her son.

13. Stabat Mater

"We leave behind a bit of ourselves wherever we have been."
                                                    —Haraucourt

CHRISTOS KNEW WHAT HE WANTED WHEN HE WENT SEARCHING for a bride. Aside from finding someone he could love, it was important that she be a virgin. She had to be mindful of her obligations to his parents and know there would be no equality in the marriage. For him, that much was expected, though never verbally articulated. It was simply understood.

And as often happened when couples were united with little prior knowledge of each other, expectations were realized because both parties took their commitment seriously. For them, a wedding contract did not include a trial period with an option to walk away. A marriage was entered into with every expectation of success. And for that reason, more often than not, it did succeed.

Christos was a good provider and role model for his sons. Lula, however, saw him somewhat differently. Early in their marriage, she thought his inability to reveal himself to her was because he had difficulty verbalizing his feelings. He held his emotions in check, she believed, because he was by nature a shy person. Then she realized that Christos, for all his posturing and notions of Greek manhood, carried with him the emotional baggage of an abandoned child. He was, after all, only a boy when he had been thrust into the world to fend for himself. Lula also understood that, to his way of thinking, there was but one way for a husband to head a family, and that was to mimic his own father, a prototypical, dominating figure married to a subservient woman who had borne him nine children. Although loved by his parents, Christos had never experienced any demonstrable expression of that love, and was uncertain how it should be returned. Yet, Lula never questioned his affection, for in his own way he made his feelings known.

Throughout their marriage, Lula was a good wife. She had made her husband's house a home and a family with children, all of them achievers. As her sons departed one by one, however, her role as a mother continued; for now it was Christos whose turn it was to receive the maternal solicitude denied him as a boy. More and more, Lula's time was spent listening to and dealing with her husband's increasing aches and pains, suggesting to him all along that although she was ten years his junior, he would outlive her for sure. The once independent male who had carved out an existence for himself in the wilds of Wisconsin had succumbed to the spouse he once kept at bay. And as Lula assumed a new role in their relationship, she clearly understood it had to be so.

They had long ago accepted the banality of their lives, enjoying a comfortable existence that lacked little. There appeared to have been no health issues between them except for Christos's constant complaints attributable to "arthritis and lumbago." But a particular pain persisted in his shoulder that was not relieved by over-the-counter medications. He said he needed to see a doctor, and upon seeking his son's advice was told to have an X-ray examination, which he did.

"The news is not good," his father's doctor reported to Leo. "Your dad has two 'hot spots' near the head of his right humerus, just below the acromioclavicular joint, which appear to be metastatic tumor. Could they have come from his prostate?" the voice on the phone inquired. "Anyway, he needs a workup, and I suggest scanning his other bones as well."

The implied diagnosis was cancer of the prostate with metastases, for it was known that every male in the Sarris family who lived beyond seventy-five had been afflicted with that disease. His father's complaints were real and not caused by anxiety as Lula had assumed. But first Leo wanted to speak with her about breaking the news to Christos, and to consider a course of action.

"We can't tell him what he's got," Lula said. "Please, for his sake and mine, don't let him know. He'll fall apart. Tell your father anything, but don't say the word *cancer*. Do it for me."

Leo had been taught in medical school that dealing honestly with a patient was always the best policy. After all, lives had to be reordered and contingency plans made whenever serious illness arose. And yet, who was he to tell his mother how to deal with a situation she herself would have to face day after day? There was no hard-and-fast rule, it seemed, how a given problem should be approached, and in this case he would listen to her.

Christos was happy to learn he had something called "Paget's disease"—a chronic and troublesome condition manageable with pain pills and "hormones" for his bones. Or so he was told. The big lie, which at first troubled Leo, proved in time to be the right approach for his father, who felt better once therapy began. Perhaps Christos understood that something more serious was involved than what he had been led to believe, but he never let on.

For Christos, the plan worked. It was Lula, on the other hand, who suffered most during her husband's illness, for although it had been upon her insistence that his real condition not be disclosed, it was she who worried whether his every ache indicated a spread of the disease. Hers were the anxious moments and sleepless nights, while Christos was spared the reality of his illness. And so it went for three years, until one day he fell and fractured a hip. A break had occurred at a cancerous part of his femur.

Leo flew to Wausau, Wisconsin, where his father had been transferred for surgery. There, during the recovery period, Christos suffered a massive heart attack. Leo never left his father's side, and, like an ombudsman, kept a watchful eye over his care. One week following surgery, Christos experienced excruciating abdominal pain and his blood pressure fell precipitously. Infarction of the mesentery was suspected. The surgical treatment of that condition was rarely successful, and in a patient with a recent heart attack, to operate meant a certain demise. As Leo observed the ominous tracings of his father's electrocardiogram, Lula wept.

"It hurts," Christos said.

"Can't he have something more for his pain?" she asked.

Leo knew the additional morphine about to be given might put his father into respiratory or cardiac arrest. The nurse paused and looked at Leo, who after hesitating finally nodded his approval. Christos yawned and took several deep breaths. He seemed relaxed and free of pain. Moments later, his breathing became shallow and infrequent, and his heart stopped beating.

It was known that Christos's ribs were riddled with tumor and would break if his chest were compressed. No resuscitation was attempted. Rather, a moment of peaceful resignation prevailed in the room when he died.

"You can say something to him," a nurse said. "He might still hear you."

"You're going home now, Dad. We're taking you home," Leo repeated quietly. And holding his father's hand, he began to cry.

Christos was laid to rest following the funeral service at St. Barnabas Episcopal Church, conducted by a Greek Orthodox priest who had been summoned from Chicago. As they left the cemetery, Lula thanked her boys for being with her and told them they were good sons.

"Your father has been liberated. And like Father Gregory said, he is in a place where there is no pain or sorrow. I too am free now," she added. "But the cross I carried for him the last three years has worn me down."

14. Guy Talk

"The reasonable thing is to learn from those who can teach." —*Sophocles*

THE MEDICAL PROFESSION HAS ALWAYS ATTRACTED PEOPLE who believe a medical degree automatically catapults one into a category called the *diploma elite,* described by Vance Packard in his book *The Status Seekers* (1959). Such individuals are visible throughout the medical landscape, ending up usually as poseurs of the profession—placing posture over practice. Fortunately, their number is small.

Leo Sarris was different. Status was unimportant to him if the definition meant owning a big house on the hill or being part of the country club set. At work he had little regard for rank, title, or committee membership and eschewed the institution's politics whenever possible. The quality of his performance and his work ethic were what mattered to him most. Outside the hospital he relished the anonymity his specialty afforded, anonymity that allowed freedom to explore the community in directions that held little appeal for his colleagues. And viewed as a somewhat unusual couple, he and Martha rarely found themselves on dance cards at most social events.

Without the need to hustle for patients, Leo was spared the burden of having to be seen at the right time and in the right place among the right people. He was bored by doctors who talked too much about their children or their portfolios. Instead, he preferred hanging out with an eclectic assortment of townsfolk who over the years had entered his orbit. To blow off steam and clear his head he took to the gym, where he regularly worked out with Ron Marek, a surgical technician also employed at Hamilton General Hospital.

Marek was a physical fitness freak whose idea of a good time was doing push-ups and working up a sweat. Of husky Polish stock, he was admired by most of his friends and ridiculed by others, who believed he had taken body building to the level of a religion. But to Ron, it didn't matter what people thought of fitness training. It had become a way of life for him, and he was happy to share his passion with anyone who showed interest. It was a point of pride that he often had Dr. Sarris as a workout partner.

A quid pro quo existed in their relationship. When pumping iron together, Leo was updated on events in the sports world; he reciprocated with tales of his life experiences. In Leo, Marek found the adult association he was denied growing up. At the gym one afternoon, he was approached by a Hispanic male often seen there.

"You're looking good, kid, but ain't you sweatin' a little too much?" the man began.

"No pain, no gain," was Marek's curt reply.

"Where's your buddy today, the older dude you're usually with? Where you work anyway?"

"Hamilton General. You hang around here a lot, but I never see you doing anything. Afraid of exercise, maybe?"

"I ain't afraid of nothing, man. Just tryin' to help out guys like you and make me a little livin'. My name's Hector, Hector Torres. What's yours?"

Annoyed by the intrusion, Ron gave no answer, ignoring the person who had interrupted his routine. Hoping the man would take the hint and move on, Marek looked straight ahead. But the intruder continued.

"Look, man, there's a better way to get big instead of doin' all the shit you're doin'. See that dude over there? Looks good, don't he? Think he got that way workin' his ass off like you? No way. Gettin' bulked up is easy if you're smart."

Ron was indeed smart, for he knew exactly what was going on. He was being hustled and taunted to take drugs—steroids, to be specific. He knew they were passed around at gyms by dealers preying on people looking for quick results.

"I'll make you a deal. You work at the hospital. I'll get you started, no cost to you if you get me syringes and needles. You gotta shoot the juice, you know. But it's easy once you get over the first stick. I'll show you how. Interested?"

"If you're smart, you'll fuck off," Marek answered.

Hector did not appear offended by the response. Rather, he casually left the premises, knowing there would be someone elsewhere to hit on. "Can't score every time," he said to himself.

A week later, Ron mentioned the incident to Leo.

"I hope you didn't do anything stupid. Or did you?" Leo asked.

"Think I'm crazy? In the first place, guys who do steroids don't even look natural. Instead of developing muscles with definition, most end up looking like King Kong. It's a gorilla look I can do without. What's your take on steroids, anyway?"

"There's no free ride," Sarris began. "There's a price you pay any time you start manipulating the body's physiology, short term and long term. I can list the harmful effects, but I'll just remind you that those drugs are illegal and people who deal with them are probably selling other illegal stuff as well.

"Bottom line? If someone knows of the harm he can do to himself and is stupid enough to go ahead for whatever narcissistic reason, then let him screw up his body. Hell, we've never been able to stop people from smoking or drinking, have we?"

"I guess not," Ron answered. "But there's something about that creep I don't like. I think he's trouble."

———

Although he knew it was Leo's way of teaching—by needling, probing, and sometimes asking outrageous questions—it was difficult at first for Ron to maintain his equilibrium when conversing with his partner. It was a version of the Socratic method that Leo practiced when he had students in tow. Eventually, Ron learned to give it back; at the gym, anything was fair game. "Why are you so critical of other doctors?" he once asked. "Do you wish you had gone into something else rather than medicine?"

Ron's question caught Leo by surprise. "No, I can't imagine doing anything other than what I'm doing. What do you mean, I'm so critical of doctors?"

"Just that. You rarely have anything good to say about anyone on the staff at the hospital."

"Sorry if I come across negative all the time. But you usually hear me sounding off when my frustration level has peaked after having kept my cool all day. And it just so happens that you always find me here working out when I gripe. For your information, there are plenty of fine doctors on our staff."

"That makes me feel better," Ron replied. "Now, there's something personal I want to ask you, something I've wondered about ever since I've gotten to know you. Do you think I have what it takes to be a doctor?"

Leo's face lit up. "You've got what it takes. For your information, medicine is not rocket science. Becoming a physician takes dogged determination, memorization, good judgment, a certain stubbornness, and a lot of common sense. The question is not whether you're capable enough, but whether it's too late for you to even think about trying, if that's what's now on your mind. Working in a hospital lets you see what's at the end of the road, but it's more important to understand what you have to do to get there."

"I think I do," Ron said.

"Many people say they want to go into medicine without having any idea what that means. In the first place, getting into medical school is the biggest hurdle of all. Getting in is more difficult than getting through. To get accepted, the name of the game is grades, grades, and more grades. Think about what it would be like for you to start college now and having to get one *A* after another for four years in a row. And if you fail to get in, what do you have?"

Neither spoke. Only the roar of the treadmills could be heard.

"Something to think about," Ron said.

They helped each other in three sets of bench presses with increasing amounts of weights, when Leo suggested a break.

"Come on. After getting your heart rate up, you want to sit back and relax?" Ron asked teasingly.

"Weight control isn't my goal. Right now these bones have had it for today."

"So let's talk," Ron began. "You asked me once how I got on this fitness kick. Remember? Well, it's because I've seen people in the emergency room hurt bad and not strong enough to hang on until they could be helped. It seems when it's important to be fit, like in a life-or-death situation, most people never are. Am I right?"

"I'll buy that. Stay in shape. You'll feel better and perform better, but don't believe for a minute you'll necessarily live longer. We're not all created equal, you know, in spite of what the Constitution says. Most of what happens to us, or is going to happen, has been programmed in our genes. With few exceptions, what's important, I think, is how we handle the cards we've been dealt. End of discussion. I'm out of here."

It was impossible for either of them to assess the impact their relationship had on the other. For Leo, it was clear that the time spent at the gym was a welcome diversion from his daily routine. At work, however, his demeanor toward Ron was all business, exemplifying his more exalted place in the pecking order of the institution's hierarchy. Ron Marek, to his credit, fully understood the parameters of their friendship both in and out of the hospital, and was careful not to assume anything more.

15. Caveat Emptor

"Be sober, be vigilant; because your adversary the devil, as a roaring lion, walketh about, seeking whom he may devour." —*1 Peter 5:8*

MARTHA WAS AWARE OF HOW MONOTONOUS HER LIFE HAD BECOME as the years went by. Eighteen, to be exact. For almost two decades she served an institution that had relentlessly exacted its due. Her professional life, to be sure, was rewarding even as she increasingly felt the toll imposed on her from working on the hospital's most demanding services. Her son, no longer a cause for concern, survived his teenage years and had chosen the military as a career. And for that she was grateful. Although she considered her relationship with Dr. Sarris to be on solid footing, there, too, a certain boredom had crept in. Like the suspended particle in a colloidal solution, moving neither upward, nor to the bottom, nor to one side or the other, Martha recently perceived her life as having little direction: it was as if it were going nowhere.

Such were her thoughts at the end of a tiring day when she was startled by a knock at the door. Through the peephole she was unable with certainty to identify the person on the other side, although the astigmatic view suggested the presence of a familiar face.

"It's me, Tyrone—Tyrone Butler. I've come by to say hello," a voice said.

"Come in," Martha answered as she opened the door. "But I thought you were—"

"Locked up? Yep, but I'm out now. I know Evan's not home, but I need to talk to somebody. My mother don't want me around, says I cause trouble and hates my friends hanging around the house. Truth is, I have nobody, and I can use some help. Can't get a job, nobody hires an ex-con."

Martha's instincts told her to send him away, but instead she engaged him in small talk, explaining that Evan was doing well while suggesting that he, too, might consider enlisting in the Armed Forces. She asked if he was hungry, but he dismissed the idea of food or drink. She inquired about his health and remarked how his body had developed since she last saw him and how handsome he had become. He explained that in prison everyone worked out to relieve boredom and to stay strong in order to be able to defend oneself, or to fend off unwanted advances.

"You don't know. For somebody like me, there ain't nothing on the outside I can do. It's hard to get started. No skills, no job, no money. That simple. Fact is I was hoping you'd stake me out with a little cash. I'll pay you back with interest or you can give me work to do. Don't worry, I have a place to stay and I'm clean. No drugs, nothing—here look at my arms."

Martha remembered how persuasive Tyrone could be and the influence he once had over Evan when they were growing up. As they spoke, she found it difficult to resist his request.

"I can give you a hundred dollars," she said, reaching for her purse. "Here, take this. It's not a loan, it's a gift. No need to pay me back. I know Daisy, your mother, would do the same for my boy if he was ever hurting. Take it. But don't come around again asking for more, because there won't be any more. And stay out of trouble."

After carefully placing the money in his pocket, he turned, put his arms around Martha, drew her close, and kissed her. She did not resist, aware only of the youthful arms that gripped her body. He said goodbye and walked slowly to the door, then turned to look at her, as if to say, "I'll be back."

16. Downward Spiral

"He that is down, needs fear no fall, He that is low, no pride."   *—Bunyan*

"So, SHE GAVE YOU A HUNDRED BUCKS, HUH? That means she's good for more if you play your cards right. How do you know her, anyway?" Hector asked.

"She's a good friend of my family. She's Evan's mother—you know, the Latin dude adopted by the nurse friend of my old lady? We're all close, have been since I been born. Her own kid's in the Marines now and she lives with a doctor. Lives with him for years, but they're not married. Just playin' house."

To his mother's dismay, Tyrone Butler was again spending time with Hector Torres, who had become the neighborhood purveyor of marijuana and assorted other drugs. After many arguments and hurtful shouting, Daisy Butler told her son to leave and get a job: to find a place of his own, wherever that would take him.

Eager to accommodate his "clients," and, if necessary, to provide "service on credit," Hector welcomed Tyrone into his world.

"Show her a good time," he advised. "Give her some sugar and she'll be yours."

———

According to her, an identity crisis existed among nurses. Believing that nothing benefited a sick patient more than the hands-on contact of a compassionate provider, Martha Ravitch felt that too much attention was paid within the profession to making nursing into something that it really was not. She sensed it every day in the attitudes of many of her colleagues, who dismissed the fundamental nature of their work as demeaning. Believing instead that nurses were equal to doctors in the healing cascade, they argued the case for having permission to prescribe medicines as well as for enjoying other prerogatives long considered the scope of physicians.

Some of her associates acted as clinical psychologists, concerned more with a patient's ego and id; others saw themselves as sociologists, social engineers, administrators, or any combination of the aforementioned. But worst of all were the elitists, who thought only a college degree could offer the social cachet their profession needed. To them, nursing could be anything other than that which demanded physical contact with patients or the soiling of hands.

Martha, however, had always believed there was a certain majesty in the work she was doing, that the concept of total commitment to an individual whose very existence depended on her vigilance and instant response was the type of nursing that excited her most and intensified her sense of worth. She was happy to have found her niche in a demanding area that permitted her to experience another aspect of patient care and to grow professionally. She was proud to have been able to develop the critical care nursing capability at Hamilton General Hospital—something that had been absent prior to her arrival.

Burnout—a constant threat to critical care providers—was a problem Martha Ravitch was acutely aware of, and at yearly intervals her practice had been to leave the intensive care unit for a month or two, requesting assignment to some other service in order to "recharge her batteries," as she put it. For relief from the mental and physical demands of her work, she preferred spending time on the obstetrical floor, where the infectious joy of young parents invariably worked its restorative magic.

But this year a reprieve was not to be had. The hospital administrator's zealous efforts to improve the institution's bottom line thwarted attempts by the nursing department to procure additional staff, and as tired and emotionally exhausted as she had recently become, Martha knew that for the time being she would have to stay put.

"How was my day? A day from hell," she replied. "I'm so exhausted I could sleep upright at this point. How was yours? A liver transplant to follow? Who's your surgeon? God, I'll see you sometime next week. Do you have a resident to help you or will you be stuck in the O.R. by yourself? Good. You'll need an extra pair of hands to keep up with the blood loss when that nut-case operates. Myself? I'm getting into a hot tub as soon as I hang up. Lots of luck. See you sometime tomorrow."

Martha had long felt that she and Leo were running on different treadmills going in opposite directions, unable to get off. They were near the end of their second decade at the hospital, working in their respective fields at all hours of the day and whenever their department heads requested more of them.

As conscientious professionals who had set an enviable standard for others to emulate, their work ethic and ability were known throughout the hospital, earning them the dubious reward of constant requests for their services by staff and employees when they or their families needed care. Such ego-boosting recognition played well in the early years of their careers, but with the passing of time, the added stress became oppressive. It was much easier, they believed, to function anonymously during routine or difficult situations. But more important, their trajectories bisected less frequently whenever they worked, and if free time was theirs to enjoy, one or the other was either too tired or too preoccupied to care. Such was the situation at Martha's house the evening Tyrone Butler came calling.

———

One day later and the count seemed greater
Than the day before—that is, the age I was said to be.
What did it mean
That my senses responded to stimuli brought to bear?
Bottom line,
That age is not a function of mathematics,
Or
You are as old as you want to be.

The Chinese worship my kind and others do as well.
When numbers are high and math needs jettisoning,
Be at peak performance,
Awaiting kouros—your gymnopédie.
Bet on it: he'll be there.

She wrote the poem in longhand, choosing and erasing words until she had expressed her thoughts as she understood them. And feeling no embarrassment or guilt for what had transpired the night before, Martha listened to the fitful breathing of Leo Sarris in the adjacent room as she carefully wrote. He had been on his feet twenty-four hours and would be up only after Martha herself had gone to work. Was it not his fault, to some extent, that she had fallen prey to the orchestrated advances of Tyrone Butler, who accurately surmised her readiness to be born again? That he had long neglected his partner was clear to Leo, who increasingly felt burdened by the inordinate pressures of his work. But for some time Martha had believed otherwise. Was it work he was tired from, or was he tired of her? Was it possible there was another woman?

Attempting to sort out her emotions and to understand why she had allowed herself to be seduced by so young a suitor, she dwelled at length on the contrasting image of the healthy person who had come on to her with that which was part of her daily existence—the continuous vision of illness, trauma, broken bones and bodies, burns, and every sort of malady one might encounter. Was it no wonder she easily succumbed to the advances of so handsome a figure as Tyrone Butler, for in him she saw the antithesis of everything her work had proffered. Was it not therapeutic to have experienced intimately that which nature at its best could deliver, a virile male devoid of the physical blemishes she saw every day? Recalling her tryst, she continued to write:

Locked in an embrace,
Both figures shared a space
That gave new meaning to the term
Double occupancy.

Twisted together like Medusa's hair—
Their serpentine writhing
Begged the question:
Were they two and not just one?

With synchronous breaths
And in measured motion,
Their passion endured
Until the deed was done.

———

It was a mistake and she knew it. Her indiscretion had created a situation she could have done without. She knew it two days later when Tyrone Butler returned ostensibly to ask for Evan's address, something he could have gotten with a phone call. She knew it for sure when she opened the door and saw her paramour in broad daylight, unshaven and smelling of alcohol. No flowers, no felicitous greeting.

"Let me in. I gotta talk to you."

"There's coffee ready if you'd like," Martha began. "Better still, have you eaten? Are you hungry?"

"No, just Evan's address. Thought I'd write and tell him I'm home."

Tyrone's reluctance to look directly at Martha troubled her as she wrote out his request. Instead, he stared at the pictures on the wall, as if he had never seen them before.

"Good," he said taking the paper from her. And after a lengthy pause, "I gotta ask you for something else. I need some cash."

For Martha Ravitch it was the moment she feared. Although she had told him the first time he had asked for money that it would be the last, she somehow knew it would not be. Now it was showtime—decision time—time to avoid compounding one mistake with another; she understood what was going on. If she agreed to his request, there would be no future relationship other than one of continuous shakedown, payback for services rendered. She could see herself descending a slope headed for disaster if she acquiesced.

What could the consequences be for her if she said no? Embarrassment? Yes. Humiliation? For sure. But worst of all would be the respect lost from those most important to her if Tyrone were to disclose what had happened. And if she acceded—if she dipped again into her wallet—he would certainly be back for more. She had forgotten when she allowed herself to be seduced that he was a petty criminal, one well tutored in the art of the scam.

Yet, at that moment she saw Tyrone not only as the boy she had helped raise and often thought of as her own, but also as a person needing her in ways he was incapable of comprehending. What he needed from her most was not money; it was love and direction. And in spite of feelings of remorse for having committed an act akin to incest, she wanted to embrace him, to take him in her arms again and say, "I care for you more than you know and I can help you."

But the moment precluded such a gesture. Instead, with stiff resolve she said, "I won't give you money and I'm not going to make a gigolo out of you either, so go market yourself somewhere else and leave me alone."

Without a word he left the house, slamming the door behind him.

———

Martha's symptoms began with insomnia shortly after she told Tyrone to get lost. For several months she complained of difficulty sleeping through the night and of being awake long before it was time to get up. And although she had no problem falling asleep, particularly after a glass or two of wine, she would awaken before her alarm was set to go off—alert, still tired, and finding it difficult to sleep again.

At first she ascribed the disturbing pattern to overwork or to being overly concerned about her next day's schedule. Then, other symptoms surfaced. Her appetite was gone and she began experiencing periodic anxiety attacks along with palpitations. But it was fatigue that prompted her to see an internist, who concluded after a thorough examination that her symptoms were psychosomatic in origin. Unable to pin a diagnosis on her assorted complaints, he implied her condition was not unlike that of many nurses who sometime acquire the symptoms of their patients. Martha was unclear what the doctor meant and questioned his conclusion.

Although she had taken care of Lula during the acute phase of her depression, Martha did not consider the possibility that she herself might now be suffering from a similar condition. She rejected such a notion because, as she reasoned, she didn't feel "down," believing that depressed people characteristically had an unresponsive affect and were disengaged from their environment. By contrast, she felt high at times, more agitated and aggressive than morose or withdrawn. All she needed, she kept telling herself, was medication for sleep and something to "get her going" in the morning.

Unaware that anything serious was troubling Martha, Leo Sarris believed she was simply overworked and only needed time off in order to feel better. Unfortunately, the problem was more complex than he had assumed, for she was clearly depressed, a depression that presented with symptoms of anxiety and agitation rather than of withdrawal. That misjudgment along with her own refusal to see a psychiatrist—something she claimed would have diminished her status at the hospital—set the stage for the problems that ensued.

A surefire recipe for trouble, one that threatens people who work in a stressful hospital setting, includes the availability of narcotics, sedatives, and stimulants, as well as the habit of self-medication and the eschewing of professional help. If served up alone or in combination with any of the others, these ingredients foreshadow a likely consequence—addiction—a problem not uncommon among doctors and nurses, and one that befell Martha, who had become dependent on the barbiturates and amphetamines she took to "get through the day." Seeking relief, she turned to drugs either obtained by prescription from accommodating friends or procured through ignominious means.

Martha's addiction could not be blamed on Tyrone Butler, although chronologically many of her symptoms developed after their tryst. Certainly, the psychological anlage—the psychosocial lesions she carried with her—had their beginnings long before her present illness, for as she once quipped during a light moment, "My emotional baggage could fill a steamer trunk and several pieces of matched luggage." And the contents of those containers would surely have included her apocryphal beginnings, her two failed marriages, her single parenthood, and her present cohabitation with Leo Sarris, the stability of which increasingly concerned her as she grew older. To such a backdrop one could add the single-mindedness of a driven professional committed to her work, so much so that a co-worker once told her to slow down by admonishing her: "Take it easy, honey. Institutions survive. Individuals don't."

There are many kinds of addiction, some worse than others. Drugs, work, and gambling readily come to mind. Addiction to a controlled substance is an abomination. Yet there are people, albeit not many, addicted to barbiturates and painkillers who hold down respectable jobs and function well enough to go undetected, sometimes for years. Such was the case of Martha Ravitch. She had become one of those faceless people who with a ready source of enabling "medications" was now less concerned about the proficiency of her work than with being exposed.

17. Retreat

"One word frees us all from the weight and pain of life:
That word is love."   —*Sophocles*

TIME HAD TAKEN ITS TOLL. BOTH MARTHA AND LEO had grown weary of the incessant demands imposed on them by work. They were no longer the fearless tigers who with youthful aggressiveness had challenged everything and everyone at Hamilton General Hospital. Earlier in their careers they enjoyed the adrenaline rush brought on during moments of life-threatening situations, and were unfazed by inordinate workloads tossed at them by senior colleagues. Recently, however, they saw themselves more as ravaged victims of some voracious and unrelenting animal.

Having worked in high-voltage areas of the hospital since her arrival, Martha requested and obtained a transfer to the outpatient clinics, where the pace was measured and a better fit for her impaired capabilities. Moreover, she welcomed working in a location that afforded cover and minimal scrutiny.

At the same time, Dr. Leo was discovering that his specialty was not an easy one in which to grow old. Although he tired now more easily, the pervasive pressure to stay current in his work never abated. And failure to do so threatened one's reputation as longer and more complex surgical procedures were developed. Because necessary surgery was rarely denied a patient solely on the basis of age or physical status, it was assumed that a good anesthesiologist could always devise a scenario that would see a patient through to a successful outcome. Put bluntly, for an anesthesiologist it meant that as he got older, his work got tougher.

Determined to maintain his skills, Leo requested a sabbatical leave in order to visit medical centers, where he could observe and put into practice newer techniques he had read about. Moreover, the opportunity to interact with other physicians was something he always enjoyed.

Unaware of Martha's addiction, Leo believed she could manage without him, now that she had been relieved of the many pressures that heretofore were hers. Besides, Daisy Butler could move in as housekeeper and companion, since her own nest had emptied.

Leonidas Sarris looked forward to a change. But the change was not one he had planned. He was needed in Eagle Creek, and it was there he would go during his leave of absence. Thoughts of updating his skills would have to wait so he could fulfill an obligation to his family.

————

The phone call from Eagle Creek came as Dr. Sarris was making arrangements for a move to London, where he had been accepted as a graduate fellow at the Royal Victoria Hospital in a program for practicing physicians. There he would be assigned a mentor responsible for his day-to-day activities, limited at first to observing in the operating rooms until he became familiar with British equipment and techniques. He was excited at the prospect of working in a hospital reputed to be tops in his specialty and by the opportunity to spend time in a foreign country. Deep in thought, he ignored the ringing until it stopped, reasoning that if the call was urgent, the phone would ring again. It soon did.

"I can't take it much longer. I need help with mother," said the voice on the other end. "We can't communicate anymore. I can't get through to her and the visiting nurse says she needs round-the-clock care. She won't eat. She moans and I don't know why. And the doctor who lives miles away is no help, only keeps telling me to put her in a nursing home. Remember, it was you who said we'd never do that to our parents."

The anguished voice was that of Leo Sarris's older brother John, who had assumed the responsibility of caring for their ageing parents following his retirement as a Greek and Latin teacher at a nearby college. A bachelor like Leo, he had become the *paterfamilias,* sparing his siblings any hands-on involvement with Christos and Lula. After the death of their father, John agreed to move in with his mother, who had grown progressively more arthritic and unable to live alone. With daytime help from a home health care service, the task of caring for Lula was initially manageable, but as she became increasingly helpless and in need of more assistance, keeping her at home had become problematic and a burden.

And although Basil, the youngest of the Sarris brothers, involved himself when he could in the affairs of their parents, his availability and whereabouts at any given moment precluded the immediate help that was sometimes needed. As a medical officer in the Army, his priorities were of necessity focused on the demands of his career and of his growing family. It was to Leo, therefore, who was more accessible, that the older brother most often turned to for support.

Compounding the situation was Lula's gradual retreat from her environment, a condition thought by one doctor to be Alzheimer's disease, while another diagnosed a recurrence of the depression she had endured years before. Perhaps it was both. Whatever the problem, she would stare at length into space without speaking. It was almost as if she couldn't hear or wouldn't listen to anything being said. Had she suffered some kind of stroke? Nobody seemed to know.

"What can I do?" asked Leo. "Do you need money?"

"No, it's not that. It's just that I can't always figure out what Mother needs or how I can help her. She moans and I don't know if she is hurting, or if she is constipated, or if she itches, or if she is thirsty, or if she has to be diapered. I'm not sure what medicine to give her for what, what to feed her, even. I'm not sure of anything anymore. The doctor knows her only through a nurse who comes by twice a week and then reports back to him what she finds, and he makes a determination without ever having laid eyes on her. It's one big mess.

"When Mother moans and I can't tell why, well, it gets to me. At night I can barely lift her onto the commode or turn her in bed. We've got to do something. We said we'd take care of our parents at home, but I can't do it alone anymore. Would a nursing home be that bad? I'm not sure she even knows where she's at."

"I don't know what to say," Leo answered after a lengthy pause. "I was planning to leave for England in a few days. I'll call you back tomorrow. Maybe it is time."

_____

He woke up abruptly when the yellow dream of the underwater cave reappeared. Only this time he was struggling to reach the surface. Gasping for air, he sat up in bed reassured he was not suffocating as his heart pounded away. He was troubled and a decision had to be made. There was still time to assess the situation before leaving for London. How could he go away for six months, he thought, without knowing what was happening in Eagle Creek? He had to find out.

Expecting to be gone only a few days, he packed a small bag and took a taxi to the airport for the flight to Chicago, transferring later to a commuter plane for the trip to Wausau, where a rental car was waiting. Within a few hours he was at the doorstep of the house, whose sidewalks as a boy he considered adversarial; for after every snowstorm—and there were many each year—he and his brothers were required to shovel the walks in the morning before going to school. It was a winter ritual familiar to anyone growing up in northern Wisconsin.

Upon entering the house, he was greeted by John and a nurse's aide. "She's in the living room," they said.

There she was, neatly dressed, hair combed, sitting in her chair, an afghan around her shoulders, her skin white and clear as Leo remembered it. And in her hands she held rolled-up washcloths intended to prevent contractures of her fingers, or so the nurses who attended her believed. As he bent over to kiss his mother, he noted the sweet fragrance of her body, a fragrance recalled from past embraces. Holding her gently, he whispered, "Mother, I'm here to take care of you."

Although there was no verbal response, he detected a faint movement of her lips and eyelids that blinked with comprehension as she stared ahead. Fighting back tears, Leo knew that at some level he had connected with his mother. And as he sat with her the next several hours, speaking softly, holding her hand and periodically stroking her hair, he remembered the Greek word for armchair—*polythrona*—which translates as "very much a throne." Even at that sad moment, while he observed her seated regally, Leo perceived his mother as very much a queen.

"I know she has lost weight and we can't seem to get her to eat. But do you think it's because Mother believes it's time for her to die, and that's why she stopped eating?" John inquired as the brothers spoke. "And if I try to spoon-feed her, she chokes on whatever is in her mouth. She doesn't seem able to chew well. She just coughs and retches."

Leo asked if she would drink and learned that his mother could swallow from a straw without difficulty. In fact, it was the commercially prepared liquid supplements that had been sustaining her.

"Then, we have to devise a plan that will give her what she needs in terms of fluids and nutrients through straws," Leo concluded. "Let's get a small blender that really blends and put in bits of meat, chicken, or even soy mixed with a little lentil soup, which has so much food value, and add it all to the commercial stuff you're giving her now. It can be thinned out to pass through a straw. Let's try something like that. And remember how fussy Mother always was about what did or didn't taste right. So we've got to sample the stuff ourselves to see if it's tasty enough before we give it to her."

The nurse's aide found a small, exquisite blender made in France and that evening all the elements were assembled. Leo prepared lentil soup the way he had watched his mother make it and John grilled chicken tenders. They added the milky supplement to the concoction until it was thin enough to pass through a rigid straw devised from plastic tubing found among the supplies left behind by the visiting nurses. The potion was seasoned, tested by Leo, and pronounced fit for trial. To everyone's relief, Lula drank her supper—the first of many that followed.

———

Leo's intent had been to assess the situation in Eagle Creek and do whatever was necessary before leaving for England. But shortly after his arrival Lula spiked a fever. No upper respiratory symptoms were detected. Her lungs were clear. Other signs of trouble were absent, yet she moaned continuously. When after a few days it was noted that her urine had a foul odor, the reason for her fever was obvious: she had a bladder infection.

"Damn it!" John responded, not because his mother had another problem, but because it could be addressed only by initiating a process put in place by the local home health care establishment to conform with the way medicine was practiced in the community. He knew the routine and hated it. There had to be a better way.

First, he was required to call the visiting nurse, who would arrive, when her schedule permitted, to obtain a urine specimen for the laboratory. Days later, the primary care physician would be notified of the results, whereupon he would phone a prescription to the pharmacy if it proved necessary. All told, five days to a week might go by from the onset of symptoms to the time when treatment could begin. In the meantime, the patient suffered. A house call was out of the question. On the other hand, transporting an incapacitated individual to a doctor's office, which constituted a significant hardship for the caregiver, was another matter entirely.

"I'm on my way now to the drugstore for an antibiotic," Leo said as he left the house. Within the hour he returned and began treating his mother. The next day, Lula's fever began to abate, her appetite improved, her moaning diminished, and the relief felt in the house was palpable. But after several days, a new problem arose. Now, she whimpered as if trying to speak, all the while squirming in her chair.

"I think I know what the trouble is," Leo said, examining his mother's bottom, something that would have been unthinkable for him to do had she been fully aware. "Just as I suspected," he announced. "I should have given her yogurt and acidophilus with the antibiotics. It's a yeast infection that's bothering her now. I'll have to treat that too."

If things occur in threes, as people say they frequently do, then a third problem inevitably had to surface, and it did. After one difficult transfer from wheelchair to commode, a skin tear was produced and found to be actively bleeding. Again, Lula's son, the doctor, rose to the occasion. He calmly applied pressure with a towel to the site and instructed the aide to continue applying pressure until he returned again from the pharmacy with the appropriate supplies. Leo carefully washed the wound, brought together the skin edges with adhesive strips, and covered the area with an antibiotic ointment before wrapping the forearm tightly in a bulky dressing.

"Others might have chosen to put in stitches," he said, "but this way we avoid having to transport her to the emergency room. And you know what that entails. I'll check her in the morning. The tear should be okay in a few days, but we have to be sure she doesn't bang her arm again and that the strips hold."

Then, something totally unexpected happened. The three medical problems that occurred within hours of his arrival in Eagle Creek resulted in an epiphany of sorts for Leo. His personal and intimate involvement with his mother's needs, and the satisfaction—the joy— derived from being there for her—made him realize it was in Eagle Creek that he would find the renewal he had been seeking. There, he would come full circle with his skills. He could care for and monitor the pulse and breath of another helpless human being—not one lying on an operating table, but instead one confined to a chair. Now it was for his mother that he would put his skills to good use.

He canceled his trip to England and decided to remain in Eagle Creek. He informed his colleagues at Hamilton General Hospital of his decision and told Martha to call him at any time should a problem arise. He involved himself zealously with the details of Lula's care, likening himself as the medical director of a private family facility, with John and the nursing staff as supporting cast.

"We didn't have a family of our own," Leo said to his brother, "but aren't we now doing exactly what we thought we were spared by never having had children to raise? Think about it. We bathe her, we clothe her, we worry about her and put her to bed. We toilet her and diaper her if necessary. We listen to her attempts to communicate and try to figure out what's wrong when she fusses. We not only prepare her food, but also feed her. They say that in old age role reversal occurs between parent and child. In our case, we are Mom and Dad, and Mother is our baby. Is there any difference?"

John hesitated to answer and finally said, "The difference is that when young parents grapple with problems of parenting, they do so having a bright future in mind for their child. We, on the other hand, avoid thinking about our baby's tomorrow, which we know will be a sad one, yet one we try to prolong. The process makes us feel good and gives us satisfaction. But who are we helping? What are we really doing?"

18. Rescue

"O mother, what have I left out? O mother, what have I
forgotten?"   *—Ginsberg*

HERE, LEO. TAKE IT. THE CALL'S FOR YOU. SOUNDS IMPORTANT. Says
his name is Evan Ravitch. Isn't that the boy your lady friend adopted?"
John asked.

Leo hadn't heard from Evan for months and wondered why he was
calling now. Evan had enlisted in the Marines after finishing high
school and was already approaching his first retirement eligibility. He
enjoyed military life, yet was young enough to pursue a different career
if he chose to leave the service. Evan was a good person and solicitous
of his mother. Rarely would he let a month go by without calling her.

"Good to hear your voice, Evan," Leo said. "How are you? Is everything all right?"

"I don't know," he replied. Then after a pause, he added, "When
did you last speak with my mother?"

"Maybe a month ago. Why?"

"Something's wrong at home. Mom doesn't sound like herself—
that's if I can ever talk to her. And when I do, it's like she's been
drinking. Tyrone Butler always answers the phone and says my mother
is either working or out somewhere. But I know it's a lie because when
I called the hospital asking for her, I found out she had quit her job.
What's going on? I know you told Daisy to move in with Mom so she
wouldn't be alone, but Daisy never answers either, only Tyrone. Sounds
like he's taken over the place. Is he supposed to be living there?"

"No, he isn't. Maybe he's just visiting his mother. Evan, have you
talked to Martha lately?

"I just got off the phone with her."

"How did she sound?"

"Not good."

"What do you mean, not good?"

"Not good, I'm telling you. She doesn't sound right. She talks slow and changes the subject all the time, and sometimes acts as if she doesn't even know who I am. Something's the matter with her. I know it, and one of us has got to go there and find out what's wrong. Can you go? I can't get an emergency leave unless I've got a good reason, like a bad accident, or somebody died."

" I'll call her when we hang up," Leo said. "You don't think she started drinking, do you? But that doesn't sound like her."

After several attempts to reach the house, Leo was finally able to get through. Tyrone answered the phone, and before either could say much to the other, Leo heard someone coughing in the background.

"Who's calling?" the person inquired.

Leo Sarris recognized Martha's voice and directed Tyrone to give her the phone. But he insisted she wouldn't speak to anyone.

"Put her on. I want to talk to her," Leo ordered.

"Man, I'm telling you she don't want to talk to nobody."

She wouldn't speak or she couldn't speak—which was it? Either way, Leo had to find out.

———

If he had known Martha was abusing drugs, he would not have remained in Eagle Creek as long as he did. What began as a response to a brother's call for help turned into a unique opportunity for Leo to commit to his mother. Now, however, he needed to turn his attention to Martha, who was in trouble. Speculating on the nature of her problem, he hurried home, catching the first available flight from Wausau.

A painful and unexpected situation awaited him on his arrival at the house. He rang the doorbell, but there was no answer. He banged on the door, still no response. Then he remembered a key kept hidden behind a loose brick for emergency use. It was still there. Opening the door, he entered and heard music coming from the kitchen. Was it the radio Martha listened to every morning before going to work? It was midafternoon now. Had she forgotten to turn it off? Walking into the kitchen, he looked aghast at the accumulation of dirty dishes scattered about—in the sink, on the stove, on the table, everywhere.

Finding no one on the first floor, he proceeded up the stairs to continue his search. There he saw two bedroom doors open, but Martha's was closed. He knocked before entering and saw her lying facedown on the covers. As he called out to her, he noted her shallow breathing. Turning her over, he attempted to arouse her, but found her unresponsive. He lifted an eyelid and observed no reflex, only a pupil, pinpoint in size. "Had she taken something?" he wondered. Then, seeing an empty syringe on the bed, he understood what had happened and sprang into action.

Leo rode in the ambulance on the way to the hospital and remained with Martha while she was admitted to the unit that had once been her domain. There she was intubated and placed on a ventilator as supportive measures were begun. Blood analysis confirmed the diagnosis of a narcotic overdose, with a drug level considered lethal. She was fortunate to have been found in time.

The ensuing days were anxious yet informative, for it was learned that Martha had quit her job and was seeing Tyrone Butler, her source of illegal drugs. Unable to abide the relationship that had developed between Martha and her son, as well as the activities she knew were going on in the house, Daisy Butler had gone to live elsewhere.

A drug-withdrawal regimen for Martha was begun after she regained consciousness, during which time she was supported by Leo and Dr. Johnson; the psychiatrist had become a family friend. Acknowledging the seriousness of her condition and the social implications involved, Martha willingly entered a rehabilitation facility with the intent of remaining there until fully recovered. Only then would she be permitted to work on nursing units where no controlled substances were dispensed.

Recognizing at the end of his emergency furlough that there was little more he could do, Evan decided to leave. At the bus station he embraced Leo as they said goodbye, thanking him for returning from Wisconsin.

"She owes her life to you and I owe you a lot myself. Try, both of you, try to get back to where you were. You and mother are my parents and I want to see you together. But just in case anything happens to Mom and I'm overseas or something like that, here, take this envelope. In it are the things she wants done when she dies."

"What do you mean?" Leo asked. "She's not about to die."

"I know, but Jewish people do things different when they do, and Mom said that even though she never went to temple much, she knew she was a Jew and wanted things carried out for her according to her religion. It's all in there. For me, she always said I should make up my own mind about what to believe."

Leo took the wrinkled envelope and put it in his pocket. Hesitating, he said, "We've had our differences and it's been tough for you at times listening to somebody who's not your real dad. But you've got to know I've tried to be a father to you."

"You have," Evan replied. "And don't forget, I've given you grief, at times, too."

Putting his arm around the young man's shoulder, Leo continued, "My own dad was proud of me, I'm sure. But for whatever reason, he could never bring himself to tell me he was. And I always wanted to hear him say it. Evan, I'm not going to make the same mistake. I'm telling you here and now that I couldn't be more proud of you than I am. So, go back to the base and don't worry about your mother. I'll look out for her."

"I know you will. But can I ask you something? Do you love her?"

Leo looked straight ahead and said, "I do—maybe more than I ever realized. I think they're calling your bus now."

19. End Game

"Each of us earns his death, his own death, which belongs to no one else, and this game is life." —Seferis

AFTER HE HAD TAKEN MARTHA TO THE REHAB CENTER, Leo Sarris began his search for Tyrone Butler, who was nowhere to be found. Obsessed by the need for a confrontation, Leo was sickened by the realization that the person he and Martha had resuscitated at birth had victimized them both. Tyrone's residence at any given moment was known by few and stood as testimony to the kind of the life he led. It was important that as a drug dealer he remain elusive.

How to find Tyrone was now the question for Leo, who concentrated his efforts on Capitol Park, an area in the center of town and minutes by foot from Hamilton General Hospital. The park, which was frequented by respectable citizens in daylight, at dusk served as a gathering place for the city's addicts, hustlers, and assorted street people. At night it was dangerous for anyone to venture there alone. Nevertheless, Leo spent hours in the area looking for his man, and by so doing allowed his face to become familiar to the lowlifes there, who wondered what game he was playing. He never stopped; he just looked. Among those aware of Leo's appearances around the park was Hector, the childhood acquaintance of Evan, and lately Tyrone's only friend.

"Why is he looking at me that way? Does he know me, or do I remind him of somebody else?" Hector Torres thought to himself. "I wonder what he wants."

Leo was not warmly greeted on his return to the hospital. Although his colleagues had sanctioned his desire for a leave of absence, they were upset by his sudden change of plans—plans they perceived as a capricious need to visit his mother. More important, they were tired of carrying his load at work. For that reason he was informed that any further delay in his return would jeopardize his position at the hospital, and a search would begin for a replacement.

What Leo had not expected was how much his ability to function effectively in the operating room had been impaired by his absence. He knew from experience that a mere two-week vacation could temporarily rob him of a certain performance edge that would return quickly, like the comeback made when getting back on a bicycle. But six months away had affected Leo Sarris's ability to stay focused and maintain the concentration his work required. He found himself fumbling at times during easy cases, feeling edgy at the slightest hint of a problem and wondering if his lapses were obvious to others. Fortunately, he had not knowingly injured anyone.

But unlike a surgeon, who has the luxury of bringing an assistant into the operating room, the anesthesiologist usually works alone, and when his confidence is shaken, the result can be frightening. Was it his prolonged absence or his obsession with what had happened to Martha that now hampered his performance? Or had the two issues collaborated to evoke the turmoil he was experiencing within himself? Whatever the reason, he knew he was in trouble, for going to work had become an unsettling experience. Under the circumstances, he worried that his once exemplary career might be marred by some unexpected disaster.

———

They had come together again, Tyrone and Hector. One, the user; the other, the abuser. Hector, the hunter; Tyrone, the hunted. Tyrone was pursued by his nemesis, while Hector pursued his habit by the only options open to him, theft and prostitution.

Lifting saleable items from stores was an art form well rehearsed and practiced by Hector, whose fence was the owner of a small neighborhood grocery store. Riskier, though often more rewarding, was his occasional foray into purse snatching. But conditions had to fall perfectly in place before he would execute an attack—namely, that his victim be an elderly woman walking alone in a space that offered a quick and sure getaway. A pickpocket artist he could never become. He was too shaky for that.

Hector found it difficult catering to the johns, who fondled his body even though he knew that servicing them was an easier way to obtain money than was breaking and entering and marketing stolen goods. But he tolerated his "clients," nevertheless, who were good for meals and clothing, and who often had jewelry or other items that could be lifted.

Tyrone sold the "good stuff" and as such was king of the park. Larger and stronger than the regulars there, he was deferred to by the acolytes that gathered around him. He did not take drugs himself and, having done time in jail, was careful to avoid any unnecessary risky behavior. Why should he be placed in jeopardy, he thought, when others would do his bidding?

"See that dude just drove by?" Hector asked. "Comes here every day lookin' for something or somebody. Just drives around. Never gets out of his car, either. What's he want, anyway?"

It was the opening Tyrone had been waiting for. Recognizing that it was Leo Sarris on the prowl, he quickly responded to Hector's question.

"I know who he is. He's a doctor I always wondered about. Lives with a friend of my old lady, the nurse that adopted Evan, the kid we grew up with. Remember him? Well, the man would be a real score if he's lookin' for anythin' from you. You ought to find out about him. He'd be good for some real money."

"Yeah, I knew I seen him before. At the gym, works out with a guy from the hospital, somebody I tried dealin' with once. But nah, he ain't lookin' for me. He seen me here plenty a times. If he interested, he'd a stopped by now. It ain't me he wants."

"Don't be so sure. He's shoppin'. That's what he's doing. Maybe he don't want to be seen pickin' anybody up at the park. Tell you what. I know he works nights every four or five days and goes home about eight in the mornin'. Walks down Elm Street to his house. Hit on him when he's by hisself. Find out what his trip is."

"Man, how do you know so much about the dude?" asked Hector.

"Believe me, I know. I've been in his house. Been with his woman, too."

———

Like a strange and silent creature peering out from beneath a rock, Dr. Sarris found himself again in the underwater cave—only this time, he was struggling to escape. It was a version of the old dream.

He was aware that his junior colleagues had been whispering that it was time for him to chuck it in, that he had lost his edge and that in the changing nature of medicine he had been left behind. But wasn't that the opinion often expressed by younger men about their seniors?

Leo had made an important decision on his own, albeit for different reasons. The stress of practice, unforgiving in its demands, was why he had decided to call it quits. He was tired and the colored dream was appearing with greater frequency.

———

Leo Sarris was exhausted when he left the hospital. He had been up most of the night on a difficult case. A young man in his twenties was thrown from a bike and brought to the emergency room, incoherent, with blood oozing from an ear and from deep lacerations of the neck. Since a CAT scan revealed no obvious brain swelling, he was transferred to the operating room for emergency surgery. The intent was to explore his neck injuries, control the bleeding, suture his wounds, and fix a broken leg as well. He smelled of alcohol and the unmistakable stench of vomit.

The problems presented by the case were numerous and serious for Leo. His first challenge would be to initiate anesthesia and secure an airway without allowing the stomach contents to be aspirated into the patient's lungs. What techniques and agents must he use to avoid swelling of an already contused brain? How should he safely manipulate and position the head and neck in order to avoid further injury? And what blood products or fluids would he administer or restrict during the case?

Bleeding from a neck wound presents a problem for any team, and

Dr. Sarris on that occasion was happy to be working with a seasoned surgeon. He knew the operation could be a long one, but was confident it would end well. And it did. After safely delivering the patient to the recovery room and giving his report, Leo joined the surgical team already assembled in the cafeteria. There, over breakfast, his thoughts turned to a theme that had been surfacing in his mind after every difficult night on call.

"A hospital like Hamilton General—a tertiary care center serving a metropolitan area, and performing, you name it, every kind of surgery twenty-four hours a day times seven weekly— is a tough place in which to grow old," he reasoned. "I can never predict what might come crashing through the door in the middle of the night, and someday, I could have a big-time disaster on my hands if I don't get out while I'm still on top of my game."

Leo was satisfied with his decision to retire, to turn a page and see what was on the other side. He wanted to go back to school and take the courses he had bypassed as an undergraduate student competing for a spot in medical school. He thought of studying a foreign language in order to prod his memory—to exercise his brain, so to speak. He wanted to sit in classrooms again, to question, debate, and compare his ability to learn alongside the bright young students of the day. He wanted to reinvent himself.

————

Revved up from the case that had kept him up all night, he knew he would find it difficult to fall asleep. As he walked along the street reconstructing in his mind the kaleidoscopic events of the past several hours, he became aware, from the cadence of the footsteps behind him, that someone was approaching. Turning around, he saw a disheveled man, his face adorned with hair and metal. A goatee and several brow piercings over the left eye appeared as noteworthy counterpoints to the dangling earrings he wore. Stepping aside as his follower advanced, Sarris paused to let the man go by.

"Hey, doc, wait a minute. Wait, I wanna talk to you."

Leo knew at a glance he was facing an addict, one who was

agitated and exhibiting the stigmata of withdrawal. Leaning into Leo as if to confide a matter of importance to him, he whispered, "I know you're a queer. My friend Tyrone says you're a faggot. You know Tyrone, the good-lookin' dude that hangs around the park. Come on. I know you and him are doin' it, gettin' it on. Look, man, I'm fucked up now. Gimme some money and I'll split. Gimme some money or I'll shoot my mouth off about you."

Leo kept walking, ignoring the person tugging at his sleeve.

"I need some dope, man, I need it bad," he continued. "Gimme a script, anyway."

The doctor stopped, and in an ill-advised moment pushed the man to the ground. Leo was in no mood to tolerate the insults leveled at him. He had just finished a difficult night on call and was not about to be hassled.

"Who the hell do you think you're talking to, you scumbag? You don't have any idea who I am. What makes you think I have anything with me, you stinking piece of shit?" Sarris fired back, his anger mounting. "I don't have drugs—you don't see me carrying a black bag, do you?"

"Don't fuck with me," the man said as he got up. "I know you're a doctor. You're Butler's john, so shut the fuck up and write me a script or gimme some money, you asshole."

In all of the years Leo Sarris had walked to and from the hospital, he had never been in a similar situation, although he knew one day he might be. He had rehearsed in his mind what he would do under such circumstances, but now, exhausted from work, he was not thinking clearly.

"I'll ask you one more time," the man said slowly, speaking through his teeth, his face expressionless and cold. "Don't fuck with me. I'm hurtin'. You're supposed to help people. What kind of no good bastard doctor are you?" he asked.

It seemed the intensity of the encounter was abating, as though the addict was listening to reason while slowly stepping back from Leo, who had turned to walk away.

"I don't need this," Sarris thought to himself. Suddenly, he felt a sharp object pierce his chest from behind, causing him to cough when he slumped to the ground. The pain, though not severe, was enough to make his chest stiffen, and it was difficult for him to breathe. He knew he had been stabbed. He felt his warm blood oozing through his clothing onto the cold pavement where he lay. His muted voice and a flailing arm caught the attention of a passing car, and an ambulance was summoned.

Then, he envisioned himself swimming again underwater, coming up intermittently for air as a pervasive stillness enveloped him in a dreamlike fugue. What he saw now was not a yellow hue filtering his view, but rather a brightness never witnessed before. He perceived himself at play on a cold winter day, his hands numb and stiff, when suddenly his mother broke the silence and called for him to come into the house. Her voice, though distant, was thought to say, "Leo, you'll catch your death of cold. Put on more clothes if you want to play." Stamatia was at the door waving at the errant boy; and there, too, was Christos menacingly shaking his fist and gesturing for him to come inside. Martha was lying with him on a watery bed, drawing a blanket over them as she had done many times before. Yet despite her presence, he shivered in her arms, as Evan, in full military dress, stood at attention, watching.

In the emergency room, he was first seen by Ron Marek, who was paralyzed at the sight of his lifeless friend. Fumbling for a vein, he attempted to wrap a tourniquet around the cold arm of his mentor.

"I need help," he shouted. "For God's sake, get me some help. Hook up the monitor. Call code blue. This man is dying."

In fact, Leo Sarris was dead on arrival at the hospital, so the newspaper reported, a victim of urban violence. The murderer, well known to the police, was apprehended while attempting to use a credit card taken from the doctor's wallet. His name was Hector Torres.

The body was accompanied by Martha and Ron Marek to Eagle Creek, where a private service was attended by Leo's brothers and several others. Evan was unable to be there. At Hamilton General Hospital, the flags flew at half-mast. Sarris was buried in the family plot next to his father. Lula died the day of the funeral.

About the Author

JAMES ROUMAN was born in Tomahawk, Wisconsin and attended public schools before enlisting in the navy during World War II. After receiving undergraduate and medical degrees from Northwestern University, he became an anesthesiologist and practiced at a major urban tertiary-care center, where he was a committed teacher of medical students and physicians entering the field of anesthesiology. Long involved in the professional affairs of his specialty, the author is now retired and lives in Hartford, Connecticut. *Underwater Dreams* is his first novel.